THE DOG LOVERS' RESCUE ROMANCE SERIES BOOKS 1-6.

MIRANDA ROSE BARKER

CONTENTS

Claim Your Free Gift   vii

HEARTS IN THE RIGHT PLACE

Chapter 1	3
Chapter 2	9
Chapter 3	16
Chapter 4	26
Epilogue – Six Months Later	33

HEALING HUMAN HEARTS

Chapter 1	39
Chapter 2	47
Chapter 3	53
Chapter 4	64
Epilogue – Six Months Later	69

THE PERFECT MOMENT OF THE HEART

Chapter 1	75
Chapter 2	78
Chapter 3	82
Chapter 4	96
Chapter 5	101
Epilogue – 6 months later	103

ADOPTING DOZER WITH HEART

Chapter 1	111
Chapter 2	118

Chapter 3	123
Chapter 4	132
Epilogue – Six Months Later	139

RESCUING ROXY WITH HEART

Chapter 1	145
Chapter 2	151
Chapter 3	157
Chapter 4	161
Chapter 5	169
Chapter 6	171
Chapter 7	173
Epilogue	179

SAVING MOXIE WITH HEART

Chapter 1	183
Chapter 2	191
Chapter 3	197
Chapter 4	203
Chapter 5	209
Epilogue	213

Last Chance to Claim Your Free Gift	215
Review This Book!	217
Also by Miranda Rose Barker	219
Other Dog Lover Books Published by Creative Bookworm Press:	221
Cozy Mysteries by Miranda Rose Barker	223
About the Author	225

A Creative Bookworm Press Book
Tucson, Arizona

This is a work of fiction. Names, characters, places, and incidents are either products of the author's imagination or are used fictitiously. Any similarity to actual events, organizations, locales or persons, living or dead, is entirely coincidental.

A Heartwarming Dog Lovers' Rescue Romance

Copyright © 2022 by Miranda Rose Barker

CLAIM YOUR FREE GIFT

Dear Reader -

Thanks for reading my book!

Sign up to my mailing list to receive exclusive copies of some of my future books as well as to be notified of any new releases, giveaways, contests, cover reveals and so much more.

Just click below to claim your free book and newsletter. See you soon...

www.MirandaRoseBarker.com/newsletter

CLAIM YOUR FREE GIFT

Miranda Rose Barker

HEARTS IN THE RIGHT PLACE

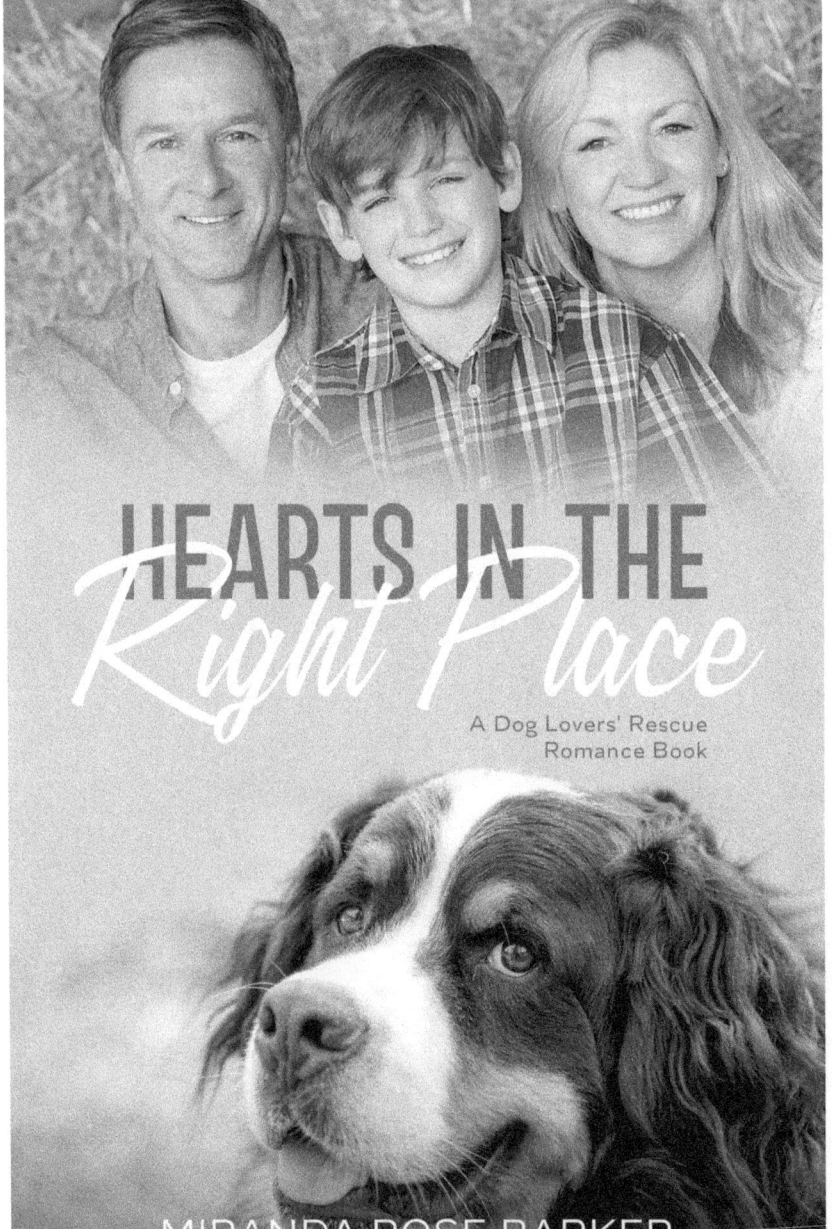

CHAPTER 1

"Hi! I'm Patty," I say when a lady named Jenn answers my call. "I heard that you have an adoption event coming up soon." I pace back and forth across the room as I speak. I can hear my sister Tamara's voice in my head as she'd said, "Patty, if Jerome needs a dog, get him one. I can help you. I'll even pay for it if you need me to. I want the little guy to be okay."

"I can afford it," I'd told her. The truth was, I'm not sure if I can, but my son needs a dog for emotional support, so I have to figure it out.

"Hey, Patty! My name is Jenn. I run the shelter and rescue. And, yes, we do have an adoption event coming up. It's this Saturday at the pet store in Bayshore Plaza. It's from nine in the morning until four in the afternoon. Do you have any idea what sort of dog you might be looking for?"

I sigh. I'm not really looking for any dog. I love dogs. I've always had a dog but, right now, I'm just so busy. I have no idea how I'll ever make it all work. My son, Jerome, wants a dog for his birthday, though. And I've foolishly promised him a dog.

"I need a dog that's good with kids. My son, Jerome, is a special-needs kid, and he needs a dog that's gentle and patient," I say reluctantly.

"Oh, well, we definitely have a few gentle souls that would probably be great for your son. How old is he?" asks Jenn.

"He's five. He is on the autism spectrum. He is very anxious, and the doctor suggested a pet might be something that helps him. My son is everything to me. I'll do whatever it takes to make his life better. And I love dogs as well. I grew up on a farm, and we always had a bunch of dogs and other animals, of course." I pause. Why was I telling this stranger about my entire life?

"I grew up with dogs, too. My dad rescued every animal that needed him." Jenn laughs.

"My dad did, too. My mom hated it, though. She was always so concerned about how clean the house was and, with dogs and kids, it never stays that way. But she tried. My sister has two dogs, and I do bring Jerome over there sometimes, but I think the doctor is right. This might help him a lot. Plus, I miss having a dog." I pause and force myself to close my mouth. Why am I so nervous about adopting a dog?

It's not like I haven't done it before. Tom and I adopted a dog when we were together, although, like everything with Tom, it was short-lived. When he left, he took the dog with him.

"Sorry, I don't mean to ramble. I just feel like sometimes the only adults I speak to are the ones I have to call to make appointments with," I say. I fidget in my chair. Why am I always so awkward?

"I get that," laughs Jenn.

"I teach kindergarten. And my son takes up the rest of the time, so… you know," I say as I laugh. It feels nice to talk to someone about something other than sippy cups and the alphabet.

"Wow, good for you. Sounds like adding a dog will be amazing for you. And, most importantly, for your son," Jenn says. "If you want, you can come and see the dogs we have here tomorrow. That way you have an idea of what we have. You can come early and apply to adopt whichever one you want on Saturday. The adoption fees will be waived that day, so it'll be a lot cheaper for you. We do have an application form to fill out, just to make sure your family and your living situation can work for the dog."

"Thank you," I say. "I'll be there tomorrow at two."

"Perfect," says Jenn.

She takes my information, and we say goodbye.

I wring my hands together nervously. Am I making the right choice? I'm not sure. Jerome is an angel of a boy, but being a single mom is a lot of work, even when your kid doesn't have special needs.

"Mom," says Jerome.

"Yes, baby," I say.

"I really want a doggy," he says. His little face droops as he says it.

"I know, muffin," I say. "We'll go tomorrow and look at the dogs."

The next day I pick Jerome up, and we head to the shelter. I can hear the dogs barking before we get to the door. Jerome is quiet next to me, his tiny hand gripped in mine.

"Now, baby, it's going to be loud in there," I tell him. He nods and bites his lip.

"We have to go in, though, and look at the dogs. Are you going to be okay?" I ask.

Jerome nods again.

Inside, we are greeted by an array of dogs barking and vying for attention. Jerome clings to my leg but remains stoic.

"Hi, you must be Patty! I'm Jenn, and this is Sarah," Jenn says to me. "And you must be Jerome."

"Hi!" I say enthusiastically. "Jerome will likely not say much. He sometimes finds situations like these to be overwhelming."

Jerome clings tighter to my leg in response.

"I understand. Let me show you the dogs," Jenn says.

The shelter has a makeshift play area in the middle of the office and another one in a corner. I see a big, fluffy dog in the center one, along with a black and tan dog with a goofy grin and a lopsided smile.

"These two here are Kelvin and Samson," says Jenn. "Kelvin is a Bernese Mountain dog, and Samson is the German Shepherd. Both of them came from families that had to give them up due to changing circumstances. Kelvin's parents got divorced, and they both moved to places where they can't have a dog, and Samson's owner passed away this year. They've been friends here ever since."

I nod. We walk to the playpen. Samson sniffs Jerome and then plants a big, sloppy kiss on him. Not to be outdone, Kelvin places his big paws on the top of the playpen and then gently places them on Jerome like he wants to hug him.

"Mommy," gasps Jerome. He holds his breath in awe.

"Yeah, baby, I think they like you!" I say. I glance at the other pen. There are three smaller dogs in it.

"I want him," says Jerome. He raises two hands and points one finger at each of the dogs.

"Maybe we want to get something a little bit smaller," I say, afraid that the fear in my voice is evident. "We live in a small house with no backyard. We would have to walk him every day, you know." I explain to Jenn. She smiles in sympathy.

"How about Mickey or Minnie?" she says. "They are the two poodles over there. Brother and sister. They were born on the street near Dallas, Texas. They've only just arrived here this week. They are very obedient already. They definitely got their mother's genes. She was a poodle. We assume purebred, but we don't know that for sure."

"Where's their mother?" I ask. Jenn looks at me sadly and shakes her head.

Right, we're in a center that rescues animals from kill shelters. I should know better than to ask that in front of Jerome.

"We also have Gina, the Springer Spaniel that's in with Minnie and Mickey. She was rescued from a puppy mill." Jenn claps her hand over her mouth and glances at Jerome. He is still mesmerized by Kelvin and Samson, and he didn't even notice what Jenn had said.

"Sorry! So yeah, she was a breeding dog, and we rescued her. She might not be the best choice for a family with kids," Jenn tells me ruefully.

"I understand," I say. "Kids can be a handful."

"So can dogs," laughs Jenn.

"Isn't that the truth!" I agree.

"We have Oscar, Sam, and Chloe in the back. Do you want to see them?" Sarah asks. "We had Stanley as well back there, but I adopted him last month. Good thing, too. We just got the news that there will be three other dogs from a rescue in Southern Arizona arriving this week."

"Wow," I say. "How many dogs will be at the adoption event?"

"We've got these eight and then another ten that are with foster families," says Jenn. "Most likely, some of the foster families will apply to keep their fosters as forever pets. That's called a 'foster fail.' We don't mind. Although, sometimes it means we need to recruit new foster families. Seems like there's a real shortage of people willing to fall in love and then give the dog back. Understandably."

"Wow," I say.

"Yeah, we've had a lot of donations lately because of a fundraiser we had. Also, one of our volunteers, Dodge, has been working around the clock to get more people involved," Jenn says. Sarah smiles and nods. If I didn't know better, I'd say she is a woman in love by the look on her face when she hears Dodge's name.

I remember how that felt. I had once had that look on my face when I thought of Tom. That was before he disappeared from my and Jerome's lives.

I force myself back to the present. "What time should we come tomorrow to the event?" I ask. Tom is gone, and I am alone with a child. The odds of me ever finding love again are pretty slim, I figure. I have neither time for nor interest in dating right now.

"You're interested in Kelvin or Samson?" asks Sarah.

I nod mutely. Jerome points and smiles at the two larger dogs.

Sarah glances at a planner in her hand. "They are the first lot that we are accepting applications on. We open at nine in the morning. If I were you, I'd arrive early. There was another man interested in both of them."

"Both of them? Someone wants to adopt two very large dogs?" I ask in disbelief.

"Yeah. He lives on a ranch outside of town. Nice guy. Lost his wife a couple of years ago, and his dog died the following year," says Jenn. "But perhaps we can convince him to take one and leave one for you."

I nod.

"Mommy, I want both," says Jerome.

"I know, babe. We'll just have to see what happens. No promises, okay?" I say. I turn to look at Jenn. "Out of curiosity, how much is it to adopt?"

"Let's see. It'll be around $300 per dog. We've waived the adoption fee, but the first round of shots and the actual vet fee for the dogs have to be paid," Jenn says. I feel the blood drain from my face.

Jenn notices and quickly adds, "It's how we stay open."

"I completely understand," I say hastily. "One dog is all we are looking for."

Jerome glares at me and bursts into tears. I pick him up, and we head back to the car.

"If we can't get one of those two, we'll get another dog, okay?"

"No, Mommy. I want those two." Jerome bites his lip in defiance. This "getting a dog" idea was supposed to help Jerome, not make him sad.

CHAPTER 2

"Come on, Jerome," I say. I glance at my watch. It's 8:30 am. If we don't leave now, we won't be there by nine. "We're going to be late, and then we won't get either dog," I tell him.

Jerome nods and continues to slowly get ready.

"Jerome! Pants, now!" I say. I take a deep breath and force myself to stay calm.

Jerome puts his pants on. I shove his arms into his jacket, and we race out the door. I toss his shoes in the back with him. I'll just carry him in. We can put them on after I make sure that we get one of the dogs.

We arrive at the mall at 8:50 am.

"Up," I command Jerome. He lets me pick him up. I race through the mall to the store, Jerome's little arms wrapped tightly around my neck as I run. I glance at the clock as I slow to a fast walk. 8:55 am.

"You made it," says Jenn. I nod as my heart pounds in my chest. Jerome looks dazed but happy. That is a good sign, at least.

"Hi, Jerome," says Jenn. Jerome buries his head against my shoulder.

"For the adoptions, we are doing a short educational session about each dog, and then you can fill out the paperwork. Do you have any idea which dog you'd like more?"

"Both," says Jerome, defiantly

"Jerome, honey," I say. "You have to pick one. Mommy can't get both."

We stop at a table at the back of the store. Both dogs are in the playpen in front of us. I plop myself down in a chair and almost gasp out loud when I glance to my right. Beside me is the most handsome man I've ever seen. He regards me coolly, his green eyes looking me over. His chiseled cheeks remind me of a rare and precious statue I once saw in a museum. When he smiles at me a second later, I feel something in the pit of my stomach that I haven't felt in a long time. Butterflies.

"Alex, this is Patty. Patty, meet Alex," Jenn says. "And this little guy is Jerome."

"Patty. Nice to meet you. I'm Alex Howe. You're my competition, then?" Alex laughs. "Just kidding. Sort of. I would love to have both dogs, but I've decided that I want Kelvin."

"I want Kelvin!" yells Jerome.

"Jerome, honey. Another outburst and we won't be able to get a dog at all today," I say calmly. I feel my cheeks flush. I know Jerome is seconds away from a meltdown. I need to act fast.

"We can always get another dog later on," I say. "Let's just get one and see how it goes."

Jerome pouts but remains silent.

"Good morning, guys," Jenn says. She stands in front of us smiling. "Now, I know the two of you have already met Samson and Kelvin, but we're going to do a little presentation on the dogs anyway in case anyone else comes in. Plus, we want to make sure that you guys are well-informed before proceeding with adoptions. We'll start with Kelvin..." Jenn turns on a presentation. On it is the large Bernese Mountain Dog.

"Kelvin is a Bernese Mountain dog. Bernese dogs are calm, sturdy, and excellent with kids," says Jenn. She smiles at me. I glance at Alex. He stares straight ahead.

"They get quite large. Kelvin will likely get to be one hundred pounds as a fully grown male. They are excellent outdoor dogs and love the cold weather. Kelvin is super-affectionate with everyone and will be great with other dogs and families alike. Berners require a lot of maintenance, though, which means they need a lot of exercise and grooming with their silky, long hair." Jenn pauses. I groan inwardly and calculate how many hours I have left in the day to be able to care for this monstrous dog.

"Berners are big on pleasing their people and can get their feelings hurt easily." Jenn smiles and pets Kelvin. He sweeps his large fan of a tail across the ground enthusiastically.

Just what I need, I think. Another overly-sensitive being to rely on me. I shake my head to get the thought out. Alex glances at me. I smile quickly. He smiles his slightly lopsided grin back, and I feel the butterflies again.

Now's not the time, Patty, I chide myself. I have enough going on in my life already. I have no business getting all fluttery about a man that is about to adopt this dog and break my son's heart.

Still, though, living on a ranch certainly paid off. Alex looked older than me, probably in his mid-forties, but the man was buff. His fitted t-shirt showcased his washboard abs and massive arms. My insides did a flip-flop.

"...Berners are usually easy to train if you start young, but I personally would recommend obedience school..." Jenn is saying. I nod absentmindedly.

Jenn finishes her presentation on Kelvin. "Any questions?" she asks.

"Yeah, when can I apply for him?" asks Alex.

"Right after the presentation. We'll be showcasing Oscar and then the poodles as well," says Jenn. "Next, we have Samson who is a German Shepherd. Shepherds are usually better in a single-dog household unless they are friends with their four-legged living mate from the beginning. In this case, though, Samson is great with most other dogs. He is also okay being alone. They are confident and loyal friends. They love their families and are great with kids. Samson here is a fully-grown male and weighs eighty-five pounds. He's strong and hearty, and he won't need as much grooming as young Kelvin. He will be fine with a quick brushing every few days. Samson will, however, be a handful when it comes to exercise. These dogs need a lot!" Jenn smiles at me.

I mentally calculate how many hours I have in the day left to walk a dog. It's not looking good, I conclude. I wonder if I can convince Jerome to fall in love with a smaller dog, one that will enjoy sitting on his lap and taking long naps.

I glance at my son. He claps his hands and grins gleefully at Samson.

"Seems like he has taken a real shine to that one," observes Alex. His deep voice catches me off-guard. I feel my insides tingle in excitement. I wonder what he would sound like saying my name in bed. I squirm in my seat embarrassed that I am even thinking this way. I am way too busy to entertain the idea of a relationship or even a fling, for that matter.

"Next up, we have Oscar. He's a wonderful Labradoodle, and he is far from a grouch. Labradoodles are mixed breeds of Labrador retrievers and poodles. They're active, family-oriented dogs that almost seem wise beyond their years. They're amazing with kids and usually with other pets. In Oscar's case, he loves everybody." Jenn pats Oscar affectionately. "The challenge with Labradoodles is that they can get bored if they don't have enough attention. They can even suffer from separation anxiety if they're left alone too long."

I glance at Jerome, hoping that he has fallen for Oscar as well, but he is sitting on the floor playing. He is not even paying attention to Jenn or the rest of the dogs. Once Jerome has made his mind up on something, it's hard to get him to change it. I sigh inwardly. Why did this man have to make my life so hard? Like I didn't have enough going on without him stealing a dog from my small child.

"Last, in this section," Jenn says. "We have Mickey and Minnie. They are a brother and sister team and, as such, we'd prefer they be adopted together. They hail all the way from southern Arizona. They were rescued off the streets of a small town in southern Arizona and brought here. Both are in excellent health, despite their challenging starts in life. Poodles are a fun breed. Like the Labradoodle, they are wildly intelligent and fairly easy to train."

I take in all the information.

"There are three types of poodles including the standard, miniature, and toy. Mickey and Minnie are standard poodles and will get to be forty to fifty pounds approximately. They are a bit thin from their time on the street, but with proper nutrition, they'll grow. They're still young, these two, and our best guess is that they're somewhere around ten months old." Jenn pauses and pats Mickey on his curly, apricot-colored head.

"Now, I'm going to turn it over to my colleague, Cole, to talk about nutrition and dogs," says Jenn.

Cole stands and begins. "Hello, everyone. Thank you for coming. In just a few minutes, we'll be opening the adoption process for these dogs. Now, any dog needs a lot of good nutrition, much like we do. Larger breeds are susceptible to hip and joint issues due to their size, although I will say that all dogs have health challenges if they are fed the wrong foods. Just like we don't eat ice cream all the time, it is important that we feed our furry family members foods that are high in nutrition and low in sugar, certain carbs, and junky fillers. A lot of the store-bought foods are filled with unnecessary non-nutritional crap. I recommend a raw diet for them or, if that's not an option for you, perhaps a homemade dog food made from whole vegetables and proteins. I make my own dog food personally because, if I won't eat it, I sure won't feed it to my dog."

My heart drops. Why did Jerome want such a big dog? I imagine the food bill and cringe. Maybe Jerome would prefer a smaller dog, one that eats less, I think to myself. I know that he has his heart set on Kelvin, though.

"Honey, I think we should consider the smaller dogs," I say. "It might be easier for Mommy to look after them and to work."

Jerome's eyes water. "But, I love the big doggies, Mommy." He whimpers. "Please? I'll be good. I promise."

My heart breaks. I sit silently fighting back tears for the rest of the presentation.

"Do you plan to apply?" asks Alex when they are done. I nod, still not trusting my voice to speak.

"I am applying for Kelvin," he says. "If you're not applying for Samson, I'll happily take him as well."

I sit there mutely, willing myself to pull it together.

"Do you need a minute?" asks Alex. Jenn stands nearby waiting.

"I … uh. I'm going to apply for Kelvin, also," I say finally. "He's the better breed for Jerome and me. Although a smaller dog would be ideal. But it's because of his anxiety. So, I have to do what's best for him." My voice sounds firm, unwavering.

Alex looks surprised for a second. "I am getting Kelvin." He says firmly. "I have a ranch. I can provide a stable life for him."

I think of the four hundred dollars in my account, which has to last until my next payday. Alex is right; he is the better choice. Still, though, my main concern is Jerome. And he wants Kelvin. So, Kelvin is the one I'm going to apply for.

"Jerome finds so few pleasures in life. I'm applying for Kelvin. May the chips fall where they may," I say. I stick my jaw out slightly in defiance. I can always ask my mom for a loan if I have to. We're not close, but she would go to the ends of the earth for her grandson. I know that, at least.

"Okay. Well, may the best man win," says Alex. He puts his hand out.

A handshake? Really? I try not to roll my eyes as I shake his smooth, firm hand.

"Alex is going to be a hard one to beat," says Sarah quietly to me as we fill out the paperwork.

"Why's that?" I ask. My voice sounds more confident than I feel.

"He is a huge supporter of the Rescue Center and is financially very well-off. He works from home a lot so he can spend hours with his adoptees. If I were you, I'd apply for Samson. Just tell Alex, and he'll leave him. He has his heart set on Kelvin for sure. He has visited him every day for the past two weeks," Sarah says.

"I want Kelvin," Jerome says. He walks over to the two dogs. Kelvin stands up and gives Jerome a hug like he did the day before. Samson licks him on the cheek. Jerome giggles gleefully. "I want them both, Mommy!" he says.

"I'm all done," Alex calls. He has a packet of paperwork in his hands.

I quickly fill out the adoption papers for Kelvin. Maybe through some weird miracle of fate, I'll get him after all. Maybe, the shelter will take pity on me.

Maybe hell will freeze over, or pigs will find themselves flying directly overhead. I know I'm about to let my son down again.

CHAPTER 3

"Mom?" I say when she picks up the phone.

"Yes, sweetie. Is Jerome okay?" my mom asks.

"Yeah. I just have a favor to ask. Can you watch him for a few hours? I need some time to sort out some work stuff." I hate lying to my mom, but our relationship has been strained ever since Tom left me, and I didn't need to make it worse by telling her I need time alone to cry.

"Yes, of course. Come by," she says.

I hang up and head to her place. "Jerome, baby, Mommy is going to drop you off at Grandma's, okay?"

"Yeah," he says. He has a glazed look in his eyes. I know he will be asleep before we get there. I drop him off and head back to the coffee shop in the center of town. Right now, I need a chai latte and a few minutes alone with my book to get my thoughts together.

Twenty minutes later, I am seated in the back corner of the shop. I gratefully hold a chai latte in my hands. The steam wafts into my face, and I smell its sweet, spicy aroma. My eyes drift closed in pure delight.

"Well, fancy meeting you here," a familiar voice wakes me from my reverie. My eyes pop open. Alex is standing in front of me, a steaming coffee in his hands. "Mind if I sit?"

He smiles at me. I wonder if he is serious. He literally just applied for the same dog my young son wants.

"Sure," I grumble.

"Listen. I want to apologize," he begins.

"Okay, why? You said you were the better choice, and I agree that you probably are," I say curtly. "I'm just a single mom trying to make my kid happy. And you're not wrong. You do have more to offer. You've made that clear."

Alex looks at me. His green eyes shine brightly, and I realize he is fighting back tears.

"I really want Kelvin, and here's why. My wife died a couple of years ago. When she was a kid, she had a Bernese Mountain Dog. His name was Skippy. She talked about Skippy until the day that she died. She died of a brain tumor. I promised her I'd get another dog someday when I was ready to return to the land of the living, and I am." Alex takes a deep breath. "At least, I think I am," he mutters.

I sigh. Well, I can't fault him for wanting Kelvin. Still, though, he was a grown man, and Jerome was just a child.

"I just want him for my son. To be honest, I have no idea how I can find the time to care for him. I mean, I can, but it seems like my entire life is a sprint since Jerome was diagnosed. You know?" I ask. Why was I telling this man about my life?

"I'm sorry," Alex says. "What was he diagnosed with?"

"He has autism and an anxiety disorder. The doctors recommended that I get a support dog for him if at all possible. So, that's what I'm trying to do," I say.

"I understand," says Alex. "I'm really sorry that we want the same pooch. Maybe you can visit him? Or I can "hire" Jerome to dog sit?" There is something about the way Alex air quotes as he says hire that makes me not hate him quite as much. His green eyes look deeply into mine. Almost too deeply.

"Yeah, maybe," I say in a noncommittal tone.

"Did you see Oscar? I bet he would love Oscar. And he's already trained," Alex says. His eyes plead with me.

"I said I'll figure it out." I don't mean to be harsh, but I'm tired. I just want to be left alone.

"Jeeze, sorry," says Alex. He frowns at me. "You must be really tired. I'm guessing that you're Jerome's sole parent?"

"I'm his mother. His dad left when we realized that Jerome had some challenges that would be lifelong. So yeah, I'm his sole parent," I retort. "Sorry. I am tired. I shouldn't have snapped at you."

Alex looks wounded for a second. "I probably said that wrong. I guess I'm not very good at this small-talk thing," he laughs. His eyes crinkle at the corners, and I feel myself longing to touch his cheek.

Stop it, Patty, I tell myself again. Am I that lonely? I don't like this man; I remind myself harshly.

"Anyway, if I get Kelvin, the offer is always there for visitation. I'd love to have you guys over sometimes," Alex pats my hand. He fishes a business card out of his pocket. "Please, call me. Any time."

I nod mutely. Alex gets up and smiles one last time. He strolls out of the coffee shop amidst stares from several of the female patrons.

"I wouldn't let that one get away," says the girl behind the counter. "And you could tell he likes you."

I smile genuinely for the first time in a long while. I might not be able to figure out how to date with my current circumstances, but it feels nice to feel attractive. I'm not sure if he really likes me or if he's just trying to make sure I wasn't an immediate enemy, though. Still, it's a nice thought, imagining someone as good-looking as he is wanting to spend time with me.

I find out the next day that I am not approved to adopt Kelvin. Jenn is apologetic and kind when she tells me.

"I'm so sorry, Patty," she says. "I tried my best to sway it your way. We ended up getting three applications for him. One of the patrons who applied for another dog also decided to apply for him. We always have to weigh and balance the dog's best interests, too."

"Who did he end up going to?" I ask. Tears sting my eyes. How am I ever going to tell Jerome?

"I can't tell you. It's confidential," she says. "But I'll give you two guesses."

"Alex?" I ask.

"I can't confirm or deny it," she says again. "But, have you considered Oscar as an option? He's a lovely guy. Trained, loyal, and great with kids. I'll even waive some of the fees as a token of our appreciation for you and your son," Jenn says.

"Why wasn't he adopted at the event?" I ask.

"He was, but then they backed out," Jenn says. "Turns out the couple adopting decided to end their marriage instead. Seems they were getting a dog as a way of saving it. I'm glad they split up before they took him home."

"Me, too," I say. "Let me talk to Jerome."

I sit beside Jerome in his bedroom that night. "Jerome, honey, we aren't able to adopt Kelvin."

"Why not, Mommy?" cries Jerome.

"Well, it seems like a lot of people wanted him. He went to another family. But," I continue hastily, "how about we go look at Oscar again? His family backed out, and now he needs a loving home. Think you could love him?" I ask.

Jerome shrugs and then smiles. "Maybe. Can we see him?"

I nod. I text Jenn to tell her we'll be there after work the next day.

"Mommy, I like the name Oscar. Like the grouch, you know," Jerome giggles gleefully. His little eyes grow large. "He's not a grouch though, right?"

"No, honey." I tousle his hair as we walk into the shelter.

"Hi!" says Jenn. I smile. A second later Alex walks out of the back with Kelvin and Samson in tow.

"Patty, what a pleasant surprise," Alex smiles at me. His face has a light stubble on it. It has a hint of gray in it. He looks rugged, handsome, and capable.

"Hi," I say.

"Here you go, Mr. Howe, all of the adoption papers are ready for both dogs," says Sarah. She follows Alex out of the back room. Sarah looks at my face ruefully. She mouths the words "I'm so sorry." I nod. I know there is nothing they can do.

"Kelvin!" exclaims Jerome and then bursts into tears. "Mommy, I love him so much."

"I know, sweet pea. But you know what?" I say. I gulp quickly. Was I really about to take Alex up on his offer? I look into my boy's sweet, puffy face, and I know that I am.

"What?" he sniffles.

"Mr. Alex said we can visit Kelvin and Samson any time. He even said you can babysit them," I exclaim. Jerome's cherub face lights up.

"Really?" he asks. He glances up shyly at Alex.

Alex looks surprised for a second but quickly recovers. "Yes, I did say that, and I would love it if you came and visited," he says. He squats down so that he is eye-to-eye with Jerome. "You can come and see me any time your mom says yes, little man," he says. Jerome looks bewildered.

"Any time?"

"Yes, but your mom has to agree first. We can't conspire behind her back, now, can we?" Alex says. He winks at me, and my heart thuds in my chest.

"Okay!" says Jerome. He wraps his arms around both dogs and falls over. Both dogs lick him enthusiastically.

"Let me help you up," I say to him. Alex also extends his hand. I am shocked when he takes Alex's hand instead of mine.

"Wow, he never does that," I whisper.

"I have a way with kids. And animals," laughs Alex as the two big dogs jump on him.

"Mommy, I want Oscar. Maybe they can all play together!" he says.

I nod, dumbfounded. Jerome is never this outgoing. He is almost always shy and plagued with worries.

"Yeah, baby. Let's do that," I say. I match his enthusiasm. "I'm just going to give Alex our number so we can go see them, okay?"

I hand Alex my number and smile. "If you're serious, call me whenever. I'll work it out." I say.

"I am serious," he says. "I would never lie to a child. Or a mother that cares as much as you clearly do."

I beam at him. "Thank you," I say, and I mean it.

Alex strides out of the rescue center with the two dogs in tow. On his way out, he stops and talks with Jenn, who is standing by the door. She nods and smiles at him as they exchange pleasantries. She pats him on the back and scratches behind the dogs' ears as they leave. I feel a small flash of jealousy when she touches Alex.

"Whoa, calm down, Sparky," I tell myself. "You're getting ahead of yourself. He's not into you. He's just being kind to Jerome. But he is nice to look at…" I conclude.

"Ready to fill out the papers for Oscar?" asks Jenn, smiling.

"Sure!"

"And I want to let you know that an anonymous donor has paid the adoption fee."

"What? Why?" I ask. "Was it Alex?"

Jenn looks surprised. "No, it was the family that originally was going to adopt Oscar. They felt bad and wanted to make sure a good family got him."

My shoulders sag slightly, deflated. Of course, it wasn't Alex. That fantasy was nice for a few minutes, I think to myself. It was nice to feel wanted, even if it was all imaginary. I quickly bring myself back to reality, and we fill out the paperwork for Oscar.

"You can take him home today," says Sarah. She staples the massive file together.

"I don't need to be approved?" I ask.

"You've been pre-approved already since you applied for Kelvin," says Sarah. "This," she gestures at the brick-sized chunk of paperwork, "is just a formality."

Later that evening, we are home with Oscar. He sits peacefully beneath my kitchen table as Jerome eats his dinner.

"Mommy, can I feed him?" Jerome asks.

"Not the food you're eating. No," I say. "I'm making his food now."

I barely have a chance to get Oscar's food on the floor when the phone rings.

"Hello?"

"Hi, Patty?" I recognize the baritone voice immediately. Alex.

"Hi," I say. I clench my hands together nervously.

"I was wondering if you'd like to come over tomorrow to see the dogs. Maybe have lunch?" Alex sounds nervous, not his usual confident self.

"Sure, I think Jerome would love that," I say.

"Great. I was thinking maybe something simple for lunch. I make a mean lasagna," says Alex.

"Jerome is a bit fussy. I'll bring his food, but yeah, I'd love lasagna or whatever you feel like making. I'm not picky at all," I say. I am suddenly nervous. What am I going to talk to this man about?

"Great, does one o'clock work?"

"Yes," I say firmly. It's okay, Patty, I coach myself. I'm allowed to have a meal with someone after all, right?

"Great, I'll text you my address," says Alex. "Oh, and bring Oscar. We have lots of room here."

"We?" I ask. Did I misunderstand him? Did he have a partner? Kids?

"The dogs and me. And Clay and Macy. And all the feathered ladies," says Alex.

"Oh. Who are Clay and Macy?" I ask, bewildered.

"My pigs," Alex says gleefully.

"You have pigs?" I ask stupidly.

"Yep, sure do. Two of them. And hens for eggs. Two dogs, a cat, and a rooster named Maxwell Smart."

"Wow," I say. "What's the cat's name?"

"Lucy Potato," laughs Alex.

I laugh. "Why?"

"I don't know. She's round like a potato, I guess," he says shyly. "It just became her nickname years ago."

"Well, I'm looking forward to meeting them all," I say. "Jerome will be excited as well."

"Great. So, see you around one?" Alex says.

"For sure," I say and hang up.

My phone buzzes a second later. It's my sister Tamara calling me.

"Hey, lady, how's the battle? Can I stop by with wine?"

"Sure. Why not?" I tell her. I really want to talk to her about Alex, anyway. I wish I had a picture of him.

Tamara arrives twenty minutes later looking glamorous and young. I envy her sometimes. She is a successful entrepreneur with a doting husband and twins. She is also one of the sweetest people I know.

"Hey, lady. I brought two bottles. I'm crashing with my sister tonight!" She laughs.

"Doesn't Dave mind if you stay out?" I ask. I imagine what it's like to have a partner that wants to be with his kids.

"Not at all. He wants me to remain focused and refreshed. And sometimes that means a sippy sip or several with my sister. Plus, my company grossed over a million last quarter," she says.

"Wow," I say weakly.

"Girl, I know that look… Are you okay? Do you need money? Help? A babysitter? What? Tell me. I can help," Tamara says.

"I'm just a little overwhelmed lately," I respond. "But I'm good. I promise. If I do need help, I'll tell you."

"Okay, you know there's no shame in that, right?" Tamara says. "I'm still willing to offer you the job, too. Just tell me and it's done."

When Jerome was first diagnosed, Tamara offered me the position of marketing director with her company. I went to college for marketing and worked in the field for the first few years of my career. Through a weird series of events, I ended up as a teacher in a job I love, but it is not as financially lucrative as my previous career. But being a teacher allows me to be near Jerome when he's in school, and that is the real bonus.

"I might someday take you up on that," I say. "But I really love my job, Tamara. And I love being near Jerome all day. Maybe when he gets older, I'll leave but, for now, it's perfect."

"Okay, babe. You do you. By the way, were you going to introduce me to this handsome fellow?" Tamara pets Oscar on the head. He looks up at her affectionately and wags his tail.

"This is Oscar," I say.

"I thought you were adopting a Kevin or Kelvin or something?" Trust Tamara to remember all the details. Now I have to tell her the whole story about Alex.

"I was," I say slowly. I tell her about the last few days. She listens, quietly waiting until I'm done to speak.

"Wow, he denied my little guy the dog he wanted?" she says. "Want me to deal with him?"

"No," I laugh. "I would have had a hard time with Kelvin anyway.

Plus, he's invited me and Jerome over any time we want to visit. And he's making lunch for us tomorrow."

"Really? Like actually cooking it?" Tamara looks incredulous.

"He says so," I say.

"What's his name? Is he good-looking?" Tamara pulls out her phone. "Alex what?"

I think for a moment. "I think he said his name was Alex Howe?" I say.

Tamara stares at me for a long second. "Alex Howe? *The* Alex Howe asked you out? No way!"

"What is he, well-known or something?"

"Yeah, girl. He's the CEO and founder of one of the country's largest PR firms," Tamara says. She types quickly into her phone. "Is this the guy?"

I look at Alex on her phone screen and gape. In the picture, he is wearing a tuxedo and is obviously at some big event. His green eyes pierce me through the phone, and I feel the butterflies and the heat in my stomach again.

"Yeah, that's him," I say.

"Oh my God, look at you!" Tamara laughs. "You're all flushed and swooning over him like a cat in heat!"

"I am not!"

"You sure are!" Tamara laughs and playfully nudges me.

"He is good-looking," I admit.

"Good-looking? Girl, he won most eligible bachelor in New York State three years running!"

"What? He did? Oh, gosh. I can't have lunch with this guy. Also, what's he doing living out here in such a small town? Shouldn't he be in New York City or somewhere?" I ask.

Tamara nods. "He was. And then his wife got sick. He sold his condo in the Big Apple and moved full time to his ranch or farm or whatever he calls it. He's semi-retired now, but he still oversees some of the work done at his company."

"Retired? How old is he?" I ask.

"Relax. He's like forty-two or something. I don't know, but if you really want to know Google can tell you," Tamara pauses. "Here's a picture I'm sure you'll like."

She turns her phone toward me. I exhale sharply. Alex is shirtless and running down the beach with his dog. It looks like it's somewhere in the Caribbean.

"Wow, what the heck?" I ask. "When was this taken?"

"He was in some magazine discussing his health-conscious lifestyle, and they used this picture and a few others," Tamara says. She scrolls through several other pictures of Alex working out and smiling at the head of a boardroom table.

"I can't go see this guy!" I exclaim.

"Wait, why?" asks Tamara.

"It's all just a little much. I'm a divorced kindergarten teacher with a five-year-old," I say.

"Well, he obviously wants to see you," says Tamara. "He even told you all about his farm. You got more detail than the magazine did."

"Oh, my gosh. Give me more wine. I can't handle this," I laugh. "At least that explains why everyone in the coffee shop was staring."

"It sure does. Yeah, you can handle this. You're a smart, wonderful woman, Patty. And anyway, he invited you for lunch, not to move in."

CHAPTER 4

I nearly cancel three times on Alex before I finally load Oscar and Jerome into my car. I wear jeans and a cardigan sweater. I keep my makeup light and simple. I think I look good. Or at least less tired than I normally do.

"Mommy, can we see all of the animals?" Jerome asks excitedly. "Tell me again how many he has!"

"Yes, baby. And we're going to have lunch there," I say. "He has two dogs, a cat, a rooster, two pigs, and some chickens. I think that's it."

"Okay, and yay!" Jerome agrees. He cheerfully looks out the window as I drive.

I arrive half an hour later and park in front of a large ranch-style home.

"Okay, Jerome, come on, baby," I say to him. Oscar jumps out of the car and sits patiently. "Good boy, Oscar!"

"Hey, you made it," Alex's deep baritone catches me off guard, which startles me. "Sorry. I didn't mean to scare you." Alex smiles his slightly lopsided grin. His green eyes twinkle.

"It was easy to find." It was a sprawling ranch, but it was on the main road just outside town.

"Mommy! This place is huge! It's big enough for a whole dog shelter," Jerome says. He eyes Alex cautiously.

"Jerome, do you remember Alex?" I ask.

"Yeah, he adopted Kelvin. I wanted Kelvin," Jerome says. He sticks his jaw out.

"I did. And I'm sorry. That's why I need you to come and see him as often as you can. I need a big helper like you for all these animals," says Alex.

"Really?" asks Jerome.

"Yeah. I need help here. Think you can do that for me?"

Jerome's eyes sparkle in excitement. "Yes, I can. Maybe we can start a rescue shelter here for doggies. And then we can have all the doggies together, and I can help!"

Alex smiles. "Well, I already like to help out at the rescue center where we found our dogs. But I have been thinking about volunteering as a foster home for more dogs once I completely retire from work."

"Really?" I interject.

"Yeah," says Alex. "Seriously. Jerome here just nailed it right on the head."

"I want to help with the dogs, okay, Mr. Alex?" Jerome says.

"Of course! I would not have it any other way!" Alex says.

Jerome's cherubic face beams with pride.

"Let me show you around," Alex says. He takes us to the barn, and we meet the animals. Jerome is gleefully excited to be here, and he giggles hysterically as each animal is introduced to him.

"Mom! I love it here. Can we live here?" he asks me. He flaps his hands excitedly.

"No, baby. But we can visit whenever Alex lets us," I say.

Alex sits down in front of Jerome. "My little man. You can come to visit any time. I like having you here. And the dogs like it too."

Kelvin and Samson bound into the barn at that moment and kiss Jerome. Oscar jumps up and down next to them. It looks like all three of them are smiling. I can't help but grin also.

"This is amazing. Thank you," I say.

"You guys are amazing. Listen, I'm sorry I didn't leave Kelvin for you. I should have. I realize that it didn't need to be that Berner right now. I can honor my wife's memory in other ways. She would have wanted Jerome to have him."

"It's okay, Alex. We've got Oscar. He's turned out to be perfect for us," I say. "How long ago did you lose your wife?"

"Over two years ago now. I always said I'd know the time was right to move on and join the land of the living again, so to speak. And I have. I deserve to be happy. I'm still here, after all. Either way, I'm sorry if I caused you any turmoil. I guess I just made a decision, and I had a hard time changing my mind about it." Alex looks at me, his green eyes than they have ever been. They seem to pierce me in all the right places. Goosebumps erupt on my arms.

"It's okay," I say hastily.

Alex serves us lunch and, as promised, it's homemade lasagna. Jerome eats his cheese sandwich and then promptly tells me he wants to play with the dogs. He runs around the barn with the outdoor animals and then in the family room with the dogs.

"Did you know that Labradoodles are usually very active? It's so funny that Oscar isn't," says Alex.

"He has his moments," I say. "But he's a medium energy dog for a medium energy family, I guess, which is good. I can't imagine walking a high-energy pup with a lower-energy kid. Seems like it might be a challenge."

"I think that being a parent is a challenge. I can't imagine being a single one. My hat goes off to you," says Alex. His eyes crinkle.

"No kids?" I ask.

"Nope, just these guys." He gestures to the dogs and the cat. She is perched delicately on the sofa watching the dogs carefully.

"We always said we'd adopt if my wife ever recovered. And obviously we know that didn't happen. I love kids," Alex adds.

I smile at him. I imagine him as a dad with all the animals. It's a nice image.

"I'm glad you guys came over," Alex says again.

"We're glad we came also, aren't we, Jerome?"

When Jerome doesn't answer, we both glance at the floor. Beside the couch, Jerome is asleep, his head resting on Kelvin. The other two dogs lay beside him.

"Wow, he must have worn them out!" Alex laughs.

"Or they wore him out. Either way, I'm pretty grateful. His anxiety sometimes gets in the way of his sleep," I say.

"I'm sorry you two have to deal with that," says Alex. He rests his hand on mine for a second. My body reacts to his touch. I feel nervous and intensely present all of a sudden.

"It is what it is," I say. "We manage."

"You seem to do more than manage. In fact, I think you're a real inspiration," Alex says. His green eyes burn into me. He moves closer and, before I can register what is happening, his lips softly touch mine. I lean into the kiss just a little before panicking.

"I can't do this. I have him to worry about. I'm sorry, Alex," I say hastily. "Please know that I appreciate everything, but I have to think of him first."

"I don't want to get in the way of that," says Alex. "I guess I just hoped there might be room for me as well."

"I think we should go," I say. "Thank you so much for everything. I hope Jerome can see the dogs again."

"Of course. Any time," says Alex. He looks confused, maybe even a little sad.

I load Jerome into the car, and Oscar jumps in beside him.

"Wave goodbye," I say cheerfully. Jerome waves, and Oscar barks excitedly at Kelvin and Samson. They bark back in response. Alex waves back. I look at all of their faces, and all of them seem sad that we're leaving. Maybe I'm making a mistake after all.

"You just left?" Tamara asks me that evening.

"Yeah. What if he can't handle the kid?" I ask.

"What if he can? He seems to want to," Tamara says. "Why not give him a chance?"

"I don't know," I say.

I don't hear from Alex until two days later. He calls me during my lunch hour.

"Hi, Patty, it's Alex," he says smoothly.

"Hi," I say.

"I was in the barn today, and I found your driver's license. It must have fallen out when we were sitting in there or something," he says.

"Oh, gosh, you know what? It was loose in my purse because I'd shoved it in my jacket pocket and then almost forgot it when I switched jackets. Thank you so much! I didn't even notice. I sure would have, though, if I'd been pulled over or something," I say.

"Can I bring it to you tonight? Around eight?" Alex asks.

"Sure. My address is on it. But I have to go," I say. "Lunch is almost over."

Alex shows up at eight o'clock with my license. He looks handsome in his jeans and a fitted t-shirt.

"Well, I should go then, I guess," he says.

"No. Wait. Come in. Have a tea or coffee or something," I say. "I owe you an apology."

"For what?"

"For leaving like I did. I'm sorry," I say.

"Don't worry about it," Alex says.

"I was out of line. Truth is, I was scared. But I'd like to see where this can go," I say.

Alex and I talk about the animals and the farm.

"I'm planning to step down from my position at my company soon," he tells me. "I don't want to do just that, you know. I feel like there's a whole other world I could be living in, rescuing and fostering animals. Plus, I want to grow vegetables."

"Vegetables?" I ask and laugh.

"Yeah, vegetables. I love to cook," he says.

"You do?" I ask.

"Yes. Now I just need someone to cook for." He winks at me, and, for a moment, time stands still.

"Oh, well," I say with embarrassment. "I mean, I like to eat. I don't mind if you cook for me sometimes. You know, if you need someone to cook for. And you feel like cooking for me," I pause, feeling uncomfortable. I'm rambling.

I am about to say something else, but Alex puts his finger to my lips.

"Shh," he says, and his lips touch mine softly. He wraps his arms around me and looks me deeply in the eyes.

"I'd like to cook for you as often as I can. Jerome, too. If you'll let me," he whispers.

"That sounds like an offer I don't want to refuse," I let myself lean a little into him. "Yes, I'd love that."

Alex tilts my head up gently with his fingers. "Patty, I'm sorry if I came on too strong. I haven't felt so drawn to anyone since I met my wife. Forgive me for being awkward. It's been a long time. Will you let me take you out, let me get to know you? Maybe to love you? There's something about you. I knew it from the second I saw you walk into the adoption event. It scared me a little. But also, it woke me up."

I feel exposed, vulnerable, with Alex looking intently into my eyes. I smile, unsure of myself, unsure of what to say next.

"I would like that very much," I say finally. "I'm sorry. I can't remember how to do this. You think you're awkward? Well, meet me," I giggle nervously.

Alex draws me closer. His strong arms wrap tightly around me, and his lips touch mine. Again.

"Like this," he says huskily. "We do it like this."

EPILOGUE – SIX MONTHS LATER

I wander around the new foster dog space in amazement. I can't believe that he did it, just like he said he would. Alex built a whole facility on his property. It's a whole separate building, big enough to house twenty dogs. But more and more of them seem to find their way into the house.

We've fostered ten dogs so far and found homes for all of them but two.

"Don't forget I have to go out this morning and pick up three more dogs. All of them are just getting off the plane from Texas. I think it's time we have an event and find the rescue center more foster families," says Alex. "I was thinking that maybe you'd like to do some promotion for the event." Alex approaches the subject cautiously.

"Me?" I say. "I've only done bake sales since before Jerome was born," I say.

"Well, you know, a bake sale would be a good start. Do you miss getting out there with people as much? But only if you want to do this. Otherwise, I'll hire someone. I just want you to get the first crack at it if you're interested," says Alex.

Trust Alex to know that I have been thinking about changing my career, again. He always seems to know exactly what I'm thinking.

EPILOGUE – SIX MONTHS LATER

"Yeah, maybe I will," I say slowly.

Alex smiles at me. "I'd like that. Anyway, I have to go. I'll be back in fifteen with new pups."

He strolls out of the foster space. I watch his strong, muscular physique and pinch myself again. How did I end up with this wonderful, caring man? I have no idea, but I am happy. Jerome is a new dad who is present and involved. And that's all that matters.

I quickly clean the area amidst a flurry of barking.

"Gracie, Cleo! You two make enough noise for ten dogs!" I laugh. Gracie gazes up at me from her bed and barks even harder.

By the time I am done, Alex is back with the three new foster dogs.

"Meet Tina, Star, and Blaze," he says. The dogs are all black and white, and they look like each other.

"They're a mom and pups!" I gasp. The puppies are small enough to still be nursing.

"They sure are," Alex says proudly. "We saved Momma, so she can still feed these little guys."

Alex gently places all three of them in the quarantined corner pen. He lovingly pets each one before he stands back up.

"This is the best thing that has ever happened to me," he says. His voice is breathless, husky.

I wrap my arms around him and smile. "You're the best thing that has ever happened to me."

"I wouldn't have had the courage to do this without you and Jerome here to cheer me on," he says. He nuzzles his cheek against my hair. I glance down at the puppies and their mom, and I beam.

Later that day, it's chore time again. The chore list is never-ending on a farm this size.

"Jerome!" I call. "Come feed the dogs!"

Jerome bounds into the bright and airy kitchen. "Come Kelvin, Samson, Oscar!" he says. He puts their bowls down carefully, the same as he does every day.

I smile down at him. Alex walks into the room a second later and wraps his arms around me. I snuggle into him for a second. I know he is going to high-five Jerome next for a job well-done, and then he's

EPILOGUE – SIX MONTHS LATER

going to scratch each dog behind the ear, the same as he has done every single day for the last six months.

"Now, scoot everyone. I'm making a special dinner for your mama, and I need utter silence to do it." He laughs.

I giggle and punch him playfully in the arm. "Utter silence? You lost the right to utter silence when we moved in!"

"Nah, I lost that when I got Drumstick," he says. As if on cue, the rooster cries out loudly. *Cock-a-doodle-do!*

Jerome giggles hysterically. He sits on the floor with our three dogs watching them eat.

"Mommy," he says.

"Yes, hon?"

"Can we get more dogs?" Jerome asks. "Can we keep one or two more from the rescue center?"

"No," I say firmly.

"Maybe," chimes in Alex.

"What?"

"Maybe. I'm selling my company this month. I'll have more money and more time than I know what to do with. And I'm already around the ranch most of the time. Adopting more dogs might be something we can do. As long as I have help from my main man here," he tousles Jerome's hair playfully.

"Yeah!" says Jerome. "I'm a good helper!"

"You sure are," Alex says.

That night, we stand hand-in-hand in Jerome's room after we tuck him in. On the floor in Jerome's room, all three dogs snore loudly. Silently, we walk to our room, still holding hands.

We crawl into bed. The small light on my bedside table burns brightly in the otherwise dark room.

"See, we have lots of room for more animals," laughs Alex. "We have all this floor space since they all sleep with Jerome." He points to the corners of our room. "Don't we deserve loud dog snores in here as well?"

He gestures toward the floor of the large bedroom in a grand sweeping motion and makes a low growling snore sound. I laugh and push him softly. He catches me and wraps me in a bear hug.

EPILOGUE – SIX MONTHS LATER

"Don't you want snoring animals, too? Or am I enough?" he asks me tenderly. I kiss him, just because.

"You're more than enough," I whisper. "But I'm always open to more four-legged friends as well, as long as I have you by my side."

"You do, and you will," says Alex softly. "Always and forever."

HEALING HUMAN HEARTS

HEALING HUMAN
Hearts

A Dog Lovers' Rescue
Romance Book

MIRANDA ROSE BARKER

CHAPTER 1

I walk into the Dogs First Rescue Center cautiously. I hate being the new kid, even after all these years of being an adult. I'm nervous. This is the first volunteering I've done since I moved across the country. It's the first volunteering I've done since Doug died.

My first impression of this town has not been great. I've been here two weeks, and I've never felt more alone. I find people are in a hurry here, and none of them want to stop and get to know a new person. Even in the local coffee shop, a good-looking man behind me told me to hurry up when I lingered too long chatting with the barista.

"Hi," I say tentatively to the woman at the front desk of the rescue Center.

"Hi!" she says. "I'm Jenn. You must be Sarah!"

I breathe a sigh of relief. Maybe this is the best thing I can do. I love dogs, and I desperately need like-minded people. And I need to build up some confidence. Since Doug died, I've spent a lot of time alone, and I think I'm just about ready to be done with that.

"I am Sarah," I confirm. "It's nice to meet you," I say. My voice sounds shaky even to me. I smooth my hands over my fitted sweater and wonder for the seven-hundredth time if I'm dressed appropriately. Before Doug died, I made decisions easily. Now everything seems more difficult. But Doug has been dead for two years now, and it's time I walk back into the land of the living.

"So, we'll get you right in here. We have a few dogs right now that are staying here. We expanded last year thanks to a bunch of donations. We had one man in particular who donated a very large sum. You'll meet him later. He volunteers here as well. His donation allowed us to build the back area, which is now a full doggy house. That means we can keep more animals here when we rescue them. Right now, we have four dogs back there. Come on! I'll show you."

Jenn walks quickly through the office and toward the back room. I follow along after her. I'm excited to be able to do this. Maybe I'll find my community and my people here finally!

"I haven't had a lot of time to work on the details of the gala. My husband Cole and I are taking care of the day-to-day details of the shelter now, and we've been doing that since Mary left. She went on medical leave abruptly. We've been short-staffed ever since. Brad is only here part-time, and Dodge has taken over planning a lot of the event details. We're pretty grateful he was willing to do it, to be honest. We just don't have enough resources to do everything."

We walk to the back, and Jenn opens the door. I'm immediately greeted by four eager noses pushing through the gate at me.

"Hello, Oscar! Hi, Sam! Hello to you, Chloe! Good afternoon, Stanley!" Jenn sings out as she pats their expectant noses. "These are the four we have here right now. Oscar is a Labradoodle that we found wandering the streets. No Collar. No microchip. No identified family. We put posters everywhere, but no one claimed him. Sam is the little fluffy guy down there. We aren't sure what type of dog he is. We only know that he was severely abused and then sent to the local pound. We got him from there. Chloe is the Lhasa Apso. She was abandoned after she got too old to be a show dog. And the last one is Stanley. He's some sort of hound who's a goofy handful. He's chaotic , with all the patience of a big rodent and the charisma of a con artist. Which he is." Jenn laughs and affectionately pets each dog. She opens the gate, and we go in. Immediately Oscar rolls onto his back, and Stanley jumps on me. I wobble for a second and almost fall over.

"Stanley!" Jenn exclaims. "No!"

I laugh and pet him affectionately. Stanley jumps up again. This time he succeeds in knocking me over. I laugh as he stands on me and begins licking my face. Jenn watches for a second, apparently amused. She's about to pull him off me when a male voice interjects.

"I see Stanley is loving up on the volunteers again."

Jenn pulls the dog off me, and I look up. Above me is one of the most handsome men I've ever seen. His chiseled jaw, blue eyes, and full lips make him easy to look at. But I close my eyes and heave in a breath. Unfortunately, he's the guy that was rude to me in the coffee shop, which makes him so much less attractive, thankfully.

"Oh, hey, look who it is," he says. "I guess you're quieter when you have a dog sitting on you."

How rude.

Jenn looks from me to him and back. "You two know each other?" asks Jenn.

"I'm just kidding. This is the lady that made me late getting here the other day. It wasn't a big deal, though. I'm just teasing you. It's nice to meet you face to face."

I feel my eyes roll as he says it. Of course, this jerk is the man who donated the money for this room.

Jenn looks at me with sympathy. "Well, then since the two of you will be working together, let me introduce you. Dodge Armstrong, meet Sarah Lawson." Jenn smiles. I can tell she's trying to smooth the awkwardness. I consider quitting right on the spot, but she had been so excited about me helping with the fundraiser they have coming up that I just can't bring myself to do that.

"Here," says Dodge. He extends his hand to help me off the ground.

I hesitate before taking it.

"Well, if you don't want my help…" he says. I force myself to reach out and grab his hand so he can hoist me up. The truth is, if he wasn't such a smug man, I could be smitten with him.

"I'm going to let Dodge go over the plans for the fundraiser event with you. I need your expertise in marketing and public outreach. This one is a big deal. They're all big deals but this one is the one that will allow us to bring a mother and her soon-to-be pups to the Center.

Right now, she is in a kill shelter — an ordinary dog pound about an hour from here. We found out about her when one of their staff reached out to us on the sly. She begged us to find the money to bring the mom here. We managed to convince the pound to let her live for longer than planned, but we basically have to raise the money right away, or they'll euthanize her and her babies.

Dodge has been integral in arranging the fundraising for this. Now we need you to work with him to make sure there's as much public knowledge about it as possible. Ideally, we'd love to raise enough money to bring all the dogs back here, but that's a lofty dream, I think. They all have some medical needs and challenges that we'll need to address when they get here, and that, of course, means we'll need even more money." Jenn pauses. "Plus, the Center has had a hard time meeting its fundraising and grant goals since Mary left. She was the brains behind the marketing aspect."

"Wow," I say softly.

"Yeah," says Dodge. "I wish I could donate more. I've done what I can personally though. My ex-wife took me to the cleaners in our divorce."

"Oh," I say. I don't know what to say next. "I'm sorry to hear that," I say quietly, not sure how I should respond.

"Yeah," says Dodge. "All I ever did was work so that she could be happy. But she wasn't."

Dodge looks at me and, for a split second, I see the hurt in his eyes. He seems more human to me, but the moment passes quickly. He lifts his head, steels his shoulders, and any softness I saw in him is now gone.

"Let's just say I'll never be so foolish as to get married again," he concludes. "I like my freedom. And my money."

I nod mutely. What a jerk. No wonder his wife left him.

"I'll leave you two to work out the details of the fundraiser. Brad, our other employee, should be back soon to help. He's just out walking Newton and his dogs," Jenn says. She glances from Dodge to me and back. "Is that going to be okay with you guys?"

I nod. I don't know if it's going to be okay or not, but I've committed myself now, and the agency needs me. They have made that clear. Before Doug got sick, I made a very lucrative living as a marketing director for several prominent companies.

I follow Dodge and Jenn back into the office. We sit down at the largest desk and look at each other. Dodge's blue eyes stare at me intently, and I can't help but feel as if he is looking through my clothes, my skin, and right into my soul. His lips form a slight smile, and I wonder if I'm amusing him in some way. He doesn't seem to have much trust in women, I conclude. I force myself to sit up straight and look him in the eyes.

"You have pretty eyes," he says. His compliment catches me off guard. Why am I so nervous around this guy? I am good at what I do. I've sat around board rooms and directed men far more pretentious than he is. Why does he put me so on edge?

"Thanks. I appreciate it," I say awkwardly.

"So, you're a marketing guru, are you?" Dodge continues. His tone is flippant, almost as though he wants me to prove myself to him.

"I used to be a director of marketing," I say evenly. I don't want to debate with this guy. I know I'm good at what I do, even if I haven't worked since Doug passed away.

For a second, I remember the last day at my job. Doug was so sick by then that he was bedridden. My work had been slacking, and, right in the middle of a boardroom meeting, I turned on my heel and walked out. I knew I was on the verge of being fired anyway since I found it difficult to pay attention to anything except Doug.

"Where do you work?" Dodge asks me. I shake myself back to the present.

"I'm not working right now," I say. "I took some time off."

"I wondered why there was nothing when I did a web search on you," says Dodge.

"What? You web-searched me?" I ask incredulously.

"Yeah, of course." He shrugs. "I take this fundraising very seriously. I wanted to make sure you were capable of working. I didn't donate all the money I did to have it sit and do nothing." Dodge says. He smiles.

Why does he have to be such a self-important ass?

"I am very capable of doing my job!" I force myself to take a deep breath. "I took time off to mourn the loss of my husband. But I assure you, I am very capable. So you need not worry about your precious money!"

I glare at Dodge defiantly. Challenge me. I dare you.

"Whoa," says Dodge. He throws up his hands like he's surrendering to the cops. "Sorry, I didn't mean it like that!"

"It's okay," I mumble.

Dodge shows me the flyers for the event that I'll be preparing the marketing campaign for. It's a gala event with a silent auction. He has gotten some very prominent artists and companies to donate items for the event. I almost hate to admit it, but he's done a really good job on the parts he's already finished.

"Wow," I say. "I'm impressed. So, what have you done for the marketing so far?"

Dodge's face falls. "Not too much," he admits with a wince.

I look at all the information, and I have some ideas brewing already. "We need to make sure this goes down as the biggest fundraiser ever. Let's get some ads started and get some traction here. Have we cross-tagged the companies and artists that have donated? We can get their online following as well."

"Okay..." says Dodge slowly. He looks cautious, but his eyes light up, and I catch them for a second. They seem to suck me in. His entire face lightens up when he smiles.

Maybe he's not so bad, I think. I decide that I have to work with him anyway so I might as well get along with him. I can put his rudeness at the coffee shop aside. Maybe *this* is who he is.

We work diligently at creating a plan all morning. By noon, I am tired but happy. It feels good to be working again, even if it's volunteering. I'm using my skills for something far more important than increasing profits for a fancy coffee chain or perfume maker selling more of their product. It feels good to give back.

"Want to grab some lunch?" asks Dodge.

"Sure," I reply before I have a chance to think.

"Great! I know of a great little Thai place around the corner. Does that work?"

"Sure," I respond.

"So, tell me about yourself," I say, after we have ordered.

"What's to tell?" asks Dodge. "I don't know. I was born in New York. I'm a business consultant now, although I didn't start that way. My brother and I owned a restaurant, but we had a falling out. He bought me out, and I haven't spoken to him since."

"Dodge is a unique name," I say. I scoop some noodles into my mouth with my chopsticks.

"It's not my real name," says Dodge. "It's a nickname. My real name is David but, when I was a teenager, I had a Dodge Charger, and I was always late for class. I had a shop teacher who never really liked me, and every time I was late, he'd say, 'Well, well, well… look who showed up. Dodge made it to class.' It stuck with my friends, and even my dad thought it was hilarious. Eventually, everyone just called me that. Now I use it on my business cards and everywhere. Even my website has that name on it."

I smile. Maybe this guy isn't so bad after all.

"That's cool," I say. "I never had a nickname growing up. I always wanted one. But I wasn't that sort of kid, I guess."

"What sort of kid?" asks Dodge.

"The kind that people want to joke with. I was always so shy and serious. I hid in books a lot. It was easier than trying to figure out how to have a social life. I guess I wasn't very good at it." I pause and remember the incident in the coffee shop. "Maybe I'm still not."

Dodge looks at me thoughtfully with his fork poised mid-bite. His blue eyes scan me, causing me to blush. His straight teeth break into a small smile that lights up his chiseled cheeks. He has a dimple I hadn't noticed earlier. He's a handsome man. I look down at his hands, embarrassed by the thoughts in my head. His hands are rugged, and yet they look soft. They look like the hands of a man who is not afraid of hard work.

He looks strong. Capable. My mind wanders to what he must look like naked, to what kind of lover he is. Would he be attentive and caring? Or selfish and only in it for his own needs? I suspect he could be both. He seems like a man who's been hurt, one too many times.

"Penny for your thoughts?" says Dodge. My cheeks immediately get hot.

"I was just…I wanted to say I'm sorry I made you late the other day," I stammer. I can't believe I'm apologizing to this guy.

Dodge smiles again. "It's okay. I was just teasing this morning. The truth is, it's my own damn fault for being late. I should have left home earlier. I was grumpy because I wanted to do more for the Rescue, but I just can't right now. Business has been slow, and my divorce cost me a fair bit of money," Dodge says. He seems to think for a minute before continuing. "I don't want that to sound like she didn't deserve it or like it was all her fault. I'm not bitter about it. Just depleted financially right now."

"How long have you been divorced?" I ask.

"We've been apart for 3 years. The divorce was finalized last year when she decided to get married again. It was amicable, but when you have money, it costs money, I guess. I wouldn't refer to myself as the wealthy donor that the Rescue promotes me as. In fact, I'd label myself a very average supporter that happens to love dogs a heck of a lot." Dodge laughs. "I'm not sure that would fit on a business card or a plaque, though."

I giggle and feel my cheeks flush again. There are little butterflies in my stomach, something I haven't felt since Doug's illness and death.

"Dodge Armstrong. Totally average philanthropist." I laugh.

"Totally mediocre," Dodge agrees. His eyes meet mine. They crinkle at the edges as he smiles. The flutter of the butterflies in my stomach intensifies.

"This is fun," I say. "I'm glad we did this."

"Me too," says Dodge. "I'm really glad I met you."

CHAPTER 2

I HEAD BACK TO MY SMALL CONDO ON THE OUTSKIRTS OF TOWN that evening. Dodge and I have come up with a pretty good marketing plan for the gala, despite it only being a couple of weeks away. I spend the rest of the evening creating a proper logo, hashtags, and posts with Maya the pregnant dog. I connect with all the important people, and I message a handful of influencers I know to see if they will align with me and attend the event.

Dodge has also forgotten one other large detail. He hasn't booked any entertainment for the event. There is no live music, nothing to keep people invested in spending the evening. I have to move quickly. I call my brother hoping he can help me.

"Hello?" he says. He sounds like he has been working out.

"Hey, Scott. Did I catch you at a bad time?" I ask.

"No, what's up?"

"I think I need your help. I'm marketing this not-for-profit gala that's in two weeks," I start.

"Wait, what?" interrupts Scott. "You're working again? That's great! I'm so happy to hear."

"I'm just volunteering but yeah. It's nice to be doing something important."

"So, what do you need?" asks Scott.

"Live entertainment. They forgot to book a band or a singer." I say. "In fact, it seems like they've forgotten a lot of things. But anyway."

"That's why you're there! To save the day. Like always." Scott laughs. "I might be able to help. Send me all the marketing info and the dates. I'll see if I have someone available. Or several someones."

"Thanks, Scott. It pays to know someone in the music industry." I feel relieved. My big brother has always been there for me. Our parents died when I was seventeen, in a car accident. He has kept me under his wing ever since.

"Not just anyone in the music industry. You are now speaking to the head promoter at my label," Scott says.

I whoop in excitement. "You got promoted? When? Why didn't you tell me?"

Scott pauses for a long moment. "You just had so much going on," he says quietly. "I didn't want to rub my good fortune in your face."

"Oh," I say. "Well, thanks, I guess. But next time just tell me! I want to share the excitement with you."

"Next time? How far up the ladder do you think I'm going to go?" laughs Scott.

"All the way to the top, baby!" I squeal.

"Right to the big pie in the sky!" chortles Scott.

"The big pizza pie!" I laugh. Scott and I have so many inside jokes that it's hard for us to even keep track. He is my best friend. When we were kids, I drew a picture of the moon as a pizza pie like the song and had a fit when my mom told me the moon was not food. I refused to believe it. I was three at the time. Scott has teased me about it ever since.

"What else is new?" he asks when we stop laughing.

"Not much. I'm volunteering with a guy named Dodge. He seems nice," I say carefully.

"Nice as in, you-might-go-on-a-date nice or nice as in, you might enjoy doing this gig and then never seeing him again?" Scott asks.

"I don't know," I say truthfully.

"Wow, you're considering a date. That's huge. This guy will have huge shoes to fill after Doug. But I'm excited for you. I don't like the idea of you being all alone and so far away from me," says Scott.

"I'm a few hours by car and a very short plane ride. It's not like I'm in another country or something," I say.

"I know. I just wish you had someone."

"Well, thank you, I guess. Let's not put the cart before the horse, though," I say. "I'm not even sure I can picture myself with anyone else. But I'm at the point now where it might be a consideration."

Scott and I chat for a few more minutes before I let him go. He promises to get back to me about entertainment the following day.

I glance around the small, empty condo. It seems so quiet. I had relished the quiet after Doug died. I didn't want to talk to anyone or be accountable to anyone for a while. The memory of being his caregiver was too raw. But now it feels like I need more, like I want to start living again. I am not sure if I am ready for a man or not, but I am definitely going to adopt one of those dogs tomorrow!

The next day, I make true to my word and ask Jenn if I can adopt one of the dogs at the Center.

"Sure!" she says. "Which one?"

"I was thinking of Stanley," I say.

"Wow," says Jenn. "He needs quite a bit of training, but he is delightful."

"He is," I say.

"Hey, Cole," Jenn turns and yells at her husband. "Sarah wants to adopt Stanley!"

"That's great!" says Cole. He bounds into the room beaming. "I wish I could have taken that crazy devil, but we already have a full bed." Cole smiles at Jenn and, for a second, I am a witness to how much they adore one another. It reminds me of Doug and me when we met. It also reminds me of how much I want that again someday.

"You guys are really happy," I say to Jenn as we fill out the adoption papers.

"We are. It wasn't always that way. I hated him in the beginning." She laughs.

"Really? I'd never have guessed."

"Yeah. But, he grew on me," Jenn says.

Cole walks past as she says it and quips, "Like a fungus. I grew on her like a fungus."

I laugh with the two of them. I feel like I'm finally finding my people, post Doug. For the first time since he was diagnosed, I feel free and happy.

"Stanley, we need to get you some training once this gala is done!" I say a few hours later. Stanley is sitting on the floor gnawing on a bone at my feet.

Dodge and I sit at the boardroom table. I show him all the posts I've done and the people I've reached out to. Two of my influencer friends have promoted it and are confirmed as attendees.

"I don't really get this whole marketing thing," says Dodge. His reading glasses are perched on his nose, and his brow furrows in concentration. "I've been actively looking for a marketing manager for my company. Honestly, I need to get my head in the game a bit more."

I imagine myself working for Dodge and helping him build his business again. Somehow that daydream turns into him touching my shoulders and bending down to kiss my head. I flush and force myself back to the boardroom. Dodge looks at me curiously.

"Penny for your thoughts?" he prompts.

"I'm not sure if they're worth a penny," I joke.

"Well, considering your thoughts have brought overnight traction to this gala, I'd sure pay a lot more than a penny for them," says Dodge.

"Thanks," I say, and I mean it.

I gaze into Dodge's eyes. He looks into mine and, for a second, I get lost in them again. Stanley quickly brings me back to reality as he jumps on the boardroom table scattering my notes everywhere.

"Stanley!" I laugh.

"Jeeze, Stanley!" echoes Dodge.

Stanley sits on my loose notes and scatters what's left of them all over the floor. He tilts his head and looks at me, his tongue lolling out of his mouth comically. He's so funny that I can't even be angry at him.

I bend down to pick up the papers. Dodge bends to help at the same time and we gently knock heads. I grab my head and laugh. He looks at me with big eyes and then grins also.

"Sorry about that. My cranium is big," he says.

"Mine too," I grin. "Also, I'm a klutz."

We both right ourselves. The air feels thick suddenly as though electricity crackles around us. Dodge looks at me. Almost as if in slow motion, he reaches out and gently touches my head. An ache forms deep inside my body that I've not felt in a long time. His touch floods me with quick, instant desire. It confuses me, scares me even, but I like it. A desire for what? I don't even know. I just know it's a *want* I didn't even know I had.

His blue eyes crinkle at the sides as he smiles at me. I smile back, my eyes lost in his. His lips move toward mine and, when my lips touch his, it's like they were meant to be pressed together all along. He kisses me softly, tentatively. Without pretense. And then it's over. We shuffle apart, both aware of the strangeness of the situation. He feels just as awkward about it as I do, apparently.

"Sorry," mumbles Dodge.

"Don't be," I say. "Nothing like a mid-day kiss to relieve some anxiety."

"Right," laughs Dodge. "People should kiss more. Hug too."

"Agreed. Like just go around hugging and kissing. Let's normalize that in the workplace." My face is on fire.

Dodge laughs. Stanley barks as if to join in. This makes Dodge and I laugh harder.

"Stanley wants in on the action," I say. I bend my head to kiss his head and he turns his face to me. He licks me hard on the mouth. I gasp, jerk backward, and almost fall off my chair.

"Stanley! At least brush your teeth before you kiss me!" I exclaim as I wipe the dog slobber off my lips. Dodge grins and scratches Stanley behind his ears. The big dog lies down by the table, happy.

My phone buzzes with a text from Scott. He's not only found entertainment for us, but he has found me a wonderful band, one that has a large following. They are all willing to play for free for such an important event. No doubt my brother has something to do with their generosity, but I'll take it.

"Wow, my brother got us a band for the gala. Problem solved!" I exclaim.

"Great!" says Dodge.

"Now, you're certain the caterer knows all the details for the gala, right? They have the time, the date, and the deposit?" I ask.

"Yes, I told you that. Jeeze. You've asked five times!" Dodge says. "I'm not a total idiot. And anyway, Mary booked it. I just signed the papers."

"I wasn't implying you were. Sorry. I'm just crossing my t's and dotting my i's. If I hadn't asked about the entertainment, we wouldn't have any at all, remember?" I say.

Dodge looks at me coolly. I know I have upset him. I bite my lip, aware I have slipped into director mode accidentally. Dodge doesn't work for me. He is a volunteer and a donor to a great cause.

"Sorry," I say curtly. "I slipped into director mode. I apologize."

Dodge nods, and the moment is forgotten. The air is still tense around us, and Dodge leaves early. I work on creating media to promote our entertainment and influencers late into the evening. Jenn and Cole leave me the key to the Rescue Center when they go home. I leave the Center with Stanley in the wee hours of the morning, exhausted but pleased with the work I've done. I'm less pleased with how things ended today with Dodge. Hopefully, I'll get a chance to smooth things over tomorrow.

CHAPTER 3

I wake up late the next day. Stanley wakes me when he can't hold it any longer and needs to go outside. I hastily take him out. I throw on a pair of yoga pants and a baggy t-shirt. I brush my hair and run out the door with minimal makeup.

"We have some news about Maya," Jenn says to me when I arrive at the Center. I can tell by her voice she is worried.

"What is it?" I ask.

"She needs surgery. She went into labor with the puppies, but things aren't going well, and they want to do a c-section. They're going to operate today *if* we can send them a deposit," Jenn says.

"We can do that, can't we?" I ask.

"Probably, but there's more. When they did her scans to check on the puppies, they realized she has an untreated broken bone that has been there for a while. They want to fix that, too, while she's under anesthesia. All in all, it will be an expensive endeavor getting her taken care of." Jenn wrings her hands nervously.

"Well. I can donate a bit," I say. "And I'll ask my brother as well. And I'm sure the gala is going to raise a lot of money."

"I hope so. I've never done anything like this before. Mary finally gave me the budget for this year after she left, and the Center is not in very good shape. Donations have been down, and it looks like we've lost one of our huge yearly grants. She should have told me sooner, but she didn't. I'm just hoping that we can get Maya, make a lot of money at this event, and turn the whole Center around!"

I immediately take control. My old life comes pouring back to me. I am good at managing stressful situations. Or I was in my before-it-all-went-bad-life anyway. It's time I dive back into that persona. I've missed that person.

"Okay, well the first step is to get the deposit to Maya's vet. Once that's done, we'll tackle the rest. Can I see the budget?" I ask.

Jenn nods. She runs to her laptop and sends me an email.

"Where's Dodge?" I ask.

"He didn't come in today. He doesn't come every day though. He does have a higher-paying job," Jenn says.

I frown. I hope his not coming has nothing to do with our little situation last night. No sooner than I think it, the door opens and Dodge walks in. He is dressed in business pants and a button-down shirt. He looks professional. Serious. Hot.

"Sorry guys, I had a meeting this morning with my biggest client." His brow furrows. "Why's everyone looking so glum?"

Jenn quickly briefs him and then turns to me. "So, what now?" she asks.

"Why are you asking her?" interjects Dodge. His brow is raised, and, from the sound of his voice, so is his back.

"She has expertise in management. I'm a bit overwhelmed. She's delegating and prioritizing for me. Basically, she is my project manager right now," laughs Jenn.

"I see. Well, I'm here as a volunteer. Not to be pushed around," says Dodge.

Jenn frowns. "Okay, well, let us know what you're interested in doing, and we can work with that."

"I'm going to take the dogs for a walk," Dodge says. He strides past us and into the dog area. A second later, he emerges with all three dogs on leashes. Silently, he walks past us and out the door.

"Wow," says Cole. "That was awkward."

"No kidding. What happened with you two?" asks Jenn.

I drop my eyes. "I think that he took a bit of offense when I took control of the entertainment last night. I also asked him a couple of times about the caterers. Looking back, I could have approached that whole situation with more tact," I mumble.

Jenn laughs. "He'll get over it."

"I hope so. I don't feel like I'm making a lot of friends here," I explain.

"We're your friends," says Cole. I smile. I'm grateful for that, at least.

We don't have enough funds to send to Maya's vet. Once I go over the budget, we barely have enough to cover the gala expenses and the expenses at the Center. Jenn looks devastated when I tell her. I'm not sure what to do, but I know I have to act quickly. Maya's life and the lives of her puppies depend on it.

"Scott!" I say as soon as my brother picks up.

"Yeah, what's wrong?" he asks.

"I need donations. Money." I quickly explain the situation to him.

"I can help," he says. "How much do you need today?"

"Two thousand dollars," I say. "And maybe a little more before we're done. And that's just to deal with veterinary expenses and food and stuff. We're hoping to be able to bring the rest of the dogs too. The other ones at the pound. Before they euthanize them."

"Wow," whistles Scott.

"Yeah," I say grimly.

"I can donate fifteen hundred right now. Can you put some in?"

I quickly go over my own finances. I haven't worked in so long, they aren't great. I did get a little life insurance money when Doug died. And I do have a credit card, I reason. If I find a job, I can donate the rest. It just means I'll have to find a job sooner than later. It'll be worth it.

"Yeah, I can do the rest of the five thousand," I say firmly. I suck in a breath. I am not sure how I'll swing it. I just know I have to, for Maya's sake.

My brother wires the money, and I send it to the animal clinic for Maya. I do it all before I tell Jenn and Cole the good news. I emerge from the boardroom elated. Jenn and Cole are working at their desks. Both of them look worried and tired.

"Guys!" I say.

"Please tell me you have good news," says Jenn.

"The money is sent. The clinic confirmed that the surgeon will do Maya's surgery immediately. We can send the rest after the gala," I say. I smile triumphantly.

"What? How?" asks Jenn.

I tell her that my brother and I covered it. I downplay my contribution a little. Let them think he did it. I don't want the accolades; I just want to save that sweet little girl's life.

Jenn jumps up and down in excitement. Cole smiles and hugs her. I grin and stand back, basking in the happiness. I feel great, that is, until Dodge strides through the door.

"What's everyone so happy about?" he asks.

"Sarah and her brother figured out the money for Maya. Maya is going into surgery today!" says Jenn.

"That's good!" says Dodge. "Let's just hope that her luck continues into the gala. We need a lot more than five thousand for it to truly be a happy ending."

Jenn glares at him for a second. "Yeah, but it's another step in the right direction."

"Oh, it is. I agree," says Dodge smoothly. "Sarah is great at making sure everyone is taking their next step. Congratulations, Sarah. Good job," Dodge says. He smiles as he says it, but his eyes remain cool, hard.

"I just want to help the dogs," I say.

"I know," he says. "Speaking of which, where's Stanley?"

"He's in the boardroom," I say.

"Nope," says Dodge.

"What? Oh, my goodness! Where is he?" I ask.

Jenn looks at Cole, and Cole glances around the room. "He couldn't have gotten out, could he?"

"The only time the door's been open was when Dodge came in, and there's no way he got out then!"

"When was the last time you saw him?" asks Dodge.

I think back to the last hour. Stanley was definitely with me when I called Scott, but I don't remember him being there at the end of the conversation. Had he walked out? Had he somehow escaped? He's a big dog. If he were here, we'd hear him for sure.

"I... I saw him when I was on the phone with my brother," I explain.

"You don't know?" He looks at me in disbelief.

"I... I think..." I blink hard as tears sting my eyes. Jenn runs over to hug me, and Cole strides toward the dog room.

"Maybe he's in here?" he says. He opens the door. No chaotic dog. No Stanley. Dodge holds the leashes of the other three dogs.

"Stanley!" shouts Cole.

"*Woof!*"

We hear a faint bark coming from somewhere distant.

"Stanley!" I shout.

"*Woof!*"

"Where is he?" I ask. I have visions of my own dog lost nearby or eating something poisonous while I was too busy saving other dogs to notice.

"It sounds like he's in the dog room," says Jenn.

"Could he have gotten into the food closet?" asks Cole.

"Should have been locked," says Jenn. "Who was the last one in there?"

We all look at Dodge. "Did you open it?"

Dodge shakes his head no. His facial expression changes suddenly though. He looks down and shuffles his feet back and forth. "I might have," he mumbles. "I gave Oscar and the gang treats before our walk. I think I locked it." But he doesn't look very sure.

Cole runs to the closet. The door is closed, but the lock is not on. He whips open the door and there, on the linoleum floor, is Stanley. He's lying in an open 50-pound bag of dog food. The kibble bag itself is half-eaten, and the food inside is almost gone. Stanley is so stuffed he can barely move.

I sigh inwardly. I wonder if this is going to be a vet bill I can't afford. Especially now with the money for Maya's surgery on my credit card.

Stanley lifts his head and whimpers.

"Crap! I guess I'll have to take him to the vet," I sigh.

"I'm sorry," says Dodge. He lowers his head.

"Yeah, fine," I say. I look at Stanley. He tries to stand and come over to me. Instead, he sits and vomits all over the floor.

"Okay, well, I'm going to have to take the rest of the day to deal with him," I say.

"I'll come with you," says Dodge. "Please, let me help. It's my fault. And I am so sorry."

I glare at him. "Fine," I bite out. It is easier to agree than it is to disagree. "I hope that the big bag of food is all he ate."

I glance around the storage closet. There's food and treats and toys inside. I can't tell if anything else is missing.

"I think he ate some of the treats," says Jenn. "Look!" She holds up a partially chewed bag with treats.

"I hope he didn't eat too much of the packaging," I grumble. I guide Stanley to the car. He is unstable on his feet, and he throws up again just outside of the car.

"Do you want me to drive?" asks Dodge.

I'm too tired to argue. "Please."

The vet suggests we do x-rays to see if he has any blockages in his intestines. "It might tell us if he ate a lot of packaging or not," he tells us. "Don't worry. We'll take good care of him."

I nod. Dodge and I leave him with the vet. The vet decides to operate. He feels like there is too much plastic in his digestive tract, and he wants to remove it.

"It's going to cost around two thousand," he tells me.

"Can I make payments?" I ask quietly.

"Yes, we can work it out."

"I'll drop you off at home," I say wearily to Dodge. "They're operating on Stanley and keeping him for the night."

"Sarah, I am so sorry," Dodge says.

"I know," I say. I'm curt. It's not that I'm angry at Dodge. I'm really not. I'm just tired.

"Sarah, can we talk?" Dodge says.

"Yeah, if you want to come over, you can," I say. "We can have a glass of wine or something."

"Listen, Sarah, I'm so sorry I've been such a jerk. I have to be honest with you. I was intimidated by you. I saw your resume, and I was impressed with your history, even with the absence of a current regular job. You're a hell of a marketer. And we got along so well that day we worked together. I just loved it. And it scared me. I kissed you. And I really liked it. I wanted to ask you out then, but I got scared."

His face is soft, his eyes open and pleading.

"Listen, my marriage was not terrible, and I am not one to sling mud, but when it ended, it hurt. A lot. I'm terrified of being hurt again. So, it's all on me. And I'm sorry." Dodge looks at me. His blue eyes seem so human, so sad. He hardly seems like the high-and-mighty man he was being just a few short hours ago.

"I understand," I say. "Doug didn't divorce me. He died. He died way too young. Yet it still felt like the ultimate betrayal. I was so angry at him for leaving. I understand not wanting to be hurt again," I say. I can't believe I just laid my heart out like that for this guy. I wasn't sure I wanted anyone to get that close to me.

"I can't imagine," says Dodge. "I am so sorry. And I'm sorry about Stanley, too."

"I know you are. I just hope that Stanley is okay," I say.

Dodge leaves late that night. I let him take my car home. He promises to pick me up the next day so we can go and see Stanley.

The next morning, he shows up as promised, and we head to the vet.

"Stanley is doing well," the technician says. "We did pull a whole plastic bag almost out of his intestines. He ate a lot of food and a lot of the packaging, but he is going to make a full recovery."

"Thank goodness. Can I see him?"

He takes me back to the recovery area. Stanley lifts his head and wags his tail when I enter.

"Hi, buddy," I say softly.

"*Woof!*"

"Yeah, you're a good boy," I say. I scratch him under the chin and on his back. He rolls over and shows me his stitches.

"Oh, bud, I can't rub the belly," I say to him. He nods his big Elizabethan cone of shame at me.

"Silly boy!" I say, and to the technician I ask, "When can he come home?"

"The vet said in two days," he tells me.

I wander back out to the front of the office. The receptionist smiles at me. "I'll make a payment today," I say.

"Oh," she says looking confused. "The man you were with paid the whole bill so far. He said he'd be right back, by the way. He just ran across the street to get a coffee."

"He paid the bill?" I repeat. "Are you sure?"

"Yeah. He put it on his credit card. You'll have to pay for the overnight charges for the next couple of days, but he covered all of the costs for Stanley's care so far."

"Oh. Okay, thank you."

I walk outside and wait for Dodge. He appears a few minutes later with two coffees.

"Here. I thought you might need one," he says.

"Thank you," I say. I take a sip before mustering the courage to ask, "You paid the bill? That's what the receptionist told me."

"Yeah, I did. It was my fault. I want to make sure I make up for my own mistakes," Dodge says.

"I understand and thank you. I can pay you back if you want, though. I don't blame you. It's an easy mistake to make in the chaos of all the dogs," I say.

"Maybe, but it was my mistake. And I'm paying," Dodge tells me firmly. I lower my gaze.

"Thank you," I say again.

Dodge gently places his hand under my chin and lifts my head to meet his gaze. "I am genuinely sorry. And I wish I had done this the other day instead of acting the way I did." Dodge leans in close to me, his hand still gently holding my chin.

His lips meet mine. They are soft, yet masculine. I deepen the kiss. His touch feels electric, and butterflies take flight in my stomach. His tongue dances with mine, and he wraps his strong arms around me. It feels nice to be held. I wrap my arms around him. His lips graze mine, and he kisses my forehead before letting go.

"Apology accepted," I say, and we both laugh.

"When is Stanley coming home?" asks Dodge.

"Two days from now," I say. "In the meantime, we have a gala to plan."

Dodge and I work diligently for the next few days on the gala. Jenn and I decide to do most of the decorating ourselves. The ballroom we've rented for the event allows us to come in the night before to decorate. Jenn, Cole, and I pack the decorations in my trunk the day before to make sure they are all prepared.

"Cole, do you have the info for the caterer?" I ask. "Dodge forgot to give it to me, and he's working today."

"Yeah, I do. I don't have the contract, though. He has it. I haven't even seen it. He got the information from Mary."

I look at the number thoughtfully. Something inside me tells me to call and confirm everything. It seems weird to me that they haven't called us yet.

"Hi, my name is Sarah. I'm calling about the gala we're having soon. I'm calling from…"

"Of course — you're from the Rescue Center," says the caterer warmly. "I'm Charlotte. How can I help you?"

"I just wanted to confirm that everything is good to go on Saturday," I say.

"Saturday? We have you down for Sunday," Charlotte says.

"What?" Oh my gosh! Dodge! He must not have read the contract before he signed!

"We can switch the day, but we won't be able to have servers there at seven. We have too many events that day." Charlotte sounds sympathetic. I am almost in tears. Is nothing going to go right? Can Dodge not do anything he's asked to do?

"What are our options?" I ask.

I can hear Charlotte typing furiously before she responds.

"Listen, if you want, we can make sure the food arrives on site. The challenge will be the servers. We just don't have enough staff to do the service at the event as well. I can get servers there for the middle of the event, sometime around nine o'clock. I should be able to pull them from the wedding they are doing by then.

Can you find someone for the first two rounds of appetizers? It's all canapés that need to be passed around, and food stations. You have one hundred and fifty guests. Five people plus our food station chefs should be enough. More would be better but, if you can get that many, you'll be in business. And I'll send people as soon as I can in the evening." Charlotte sounds hopeful. She really is trying hard to fix a mistake that she didn't even make.

"Yes, I can work it out," I say. "Please, let's just have the food ready to be passed around at seven as we originally planned."

"We can plan on that. I'm really sorry for the confusion. Originally when Mary booked it, she wanted to do a Sunday event. I don't know when it changed, but we'll make it work. Don't worry. We don't call ourselves *Food Possible* for nothing."

I thank her profusely and hang up. I stare at my phone in a panicked rage. No wonder this shelter is having issues.

My phone rings. I see Dodge's number pop up.

"Hello?" I bite my lip, trying to keep my anger under control.

"You sound upset," says Dodge. "Is everything okay?"

"Oh, sure, just fine," I say. I can feel myself vibrating.

"What happened? Is Stanley okay?" asks Dodge. I feel my anger drop a bit. He is a caring guy. I don't know what has happened or how it happened.

"Stanley is fine. I have a question, though. How the heck did the caterers have the wrong day for the event?" I ask sweetly.

"What?" Dodge sounds alarmed.

"Yeah, so I decided to call on a whim to confirm times. And they have the date for Sunday. I've sort of fixed it, but we need to find servers to pass out food during the first half of the event. They don't have enough staff."

"Oh my god, I don't know how that could have happened," says Dodge slowly.

"Yeah, me either, but now we have an issue. We need at least five servers for seven o'clock on Saturday. Two days from now."

"Mary booked it, but I signed the contract when she went on

leave. I don't know what to say." He makes a low sound that might be coming from his throat. Or frustration. I'd wager on frustration.

"Fine. We can talk about it later. I have a lot to do now. Including picking up my sick dog," I say. I know I am being curt.

"I'll see you later, okay?" prompts Dodge. "And I am so sorry I've made so many mistakes. I guess my mind has been on my failing business and not on this. I am so sorry."

"It's fine," I say and hang up.

"What was that all about?" asks Jenn.

I tell her, and she stares at me incredulously. "Mary told me before she left that it was all taken care of."

"Yeah, it was. Just not for the right date," I say.

"Well…" says Jenn slowly. "I guess we can serve, can't we?"

"Yeah, we can. We're going to have to. Unless you know five servers looking for a gig."

CHAPTER 4

I WAKE UP EARLY ON THE MORNING OF THE GALA. The decorations went up without a hitch yesterday, and Dodge has been super-helpful and kind. I'm still angry at him, but at least he's agreeable.

I dress in yoga pants and a t-shirt and head to the conference center to deal with some last-minute preparations. Jenn, Cole, and Brad all show up with their gala-wear and catering clothes.

"Where's Dodge?" I ask. "We need him here to get everything set up."

"We're basically ready," says Jenn. "He'll be here. I know he's made some mistakes but, honestly, the food closet mishap could have happened to any one of us. The catering? Well, I should have checked the contract date. I'm as much to blame as he is."

"It's all going to work out," says Cole.

"It has to. Otherwise, we might lose the Center," I say. Not to mention Maya.

"We have to raise at least twenty-five thousand dollars for this to be considered a success," I tell them.

They nod silently.

Dodge runs in a few minutes later. We are meeting with the caterers and getting our instructions for the canapés.

"Guys! Sorry I'm late. But I have good news!" Dodge is breathless as he speaks. "I have seven servers for the event. They can stay as long as we need them."

I beam at him. "What? You mean I don't have to pass food around? Because, you know, I'm as graceful as a gazelle on roller skates."

"I fixed my mistake. Look, I should have looked at the contract more closely. Mary was sick already when she booked it. I knew the potential was there for errors. I went to my brother, to the old restaurant that I used to own. I made amends with him, and he lent me six servers. He and his wife and two kids are working tonight at the restaurant to cover the servers he gave me. But we're covered. Get out of your serving clothes and into the gala clothes. We got this, guys. No more screw-ups. I promise!" Dodge looks hopefully at the rest of us.

"You're forgiven," says Jenn.

"Sure are!" says Cole. "I have never served a thing in my life. I am certain I do *not* have what it takes to serve gala guests."

I smile at Dodge. He looks at me hopefully. "I forgave you before you brought the servers. But I'm grateful to not have to wear that hat tonight," I say.

Dodge smiles. He runs out to the hall and brings in the six servers.

I brief them quickly and introduce them to the chefs. They all seem competent and ready to work.

Jenn, Cole, Dodge, and I run back to our homes to change. I choose one of two cocktail dresses I own. The one I choose is a sparkly number from my days of working at an elegant beauty product company. It's fitted and short. I feel glamorous and a little like an imposter. I haven't worn anything fancy since before Doug got sick.

"How do I look, Stanley?" I ask. Stanley raises his head and barks. "I feel pretty good. How do you feel after your rough week?" Stanley barks again. I kiss the top of his soft head. "Are you going to be good while I'm gone?" I ask. Stanley barks and wags his tail.

I arrive at the gala right on time. Jenn and Cole are in the foyer greeting people. Brad arrives at the same time I do.

"Hi!" I say.

"Whoa," says Jenn. "Look at you! Wow!"

"You look great, girl," says Brad.

I blush and thank them. "Where's Dodge?" I ask.

"He's just parking. He just texted me," says Cole. "By the way, only half the guests are here, and we've already got some really high bids on the silent auction. That doesn't even include what we made in online donations and ticket purchases."

"Great!" I exclaim.

A second later, Dodge strides through the door. He looks handsome in his tuxedo. My jaw drops. He doesn't see me at first, as he is preoccupied with the crowd entering. Jenn waves him over. His eyes meet mine a second later. They grow wide, and then a huge smile breaks out on his face.

"Wow, Sarah," he says. "You look beautiful."

I feel myself blush. "Thank you," I murmur. "This old thing is from my days at a classy beauty company. It was a gift after one of the events I managed and worked." I feel myself rambling.

The truth is, I can't get over how great Dodge looks. He is lean and polished and shaved. His hair has been freshly cut and styled. I am giddy that he told me I look good. I feel good.

"Your servers are great. Thank you so much!" I say. "How much are they costing, by the way? I don't have them in the budget. But we will get a bit back from the caterer since they couldn't bring theirs today. Not that they have to do that, but I guess they love dogs as well." I pause. I'm aware of how fast I'm talking. I stop for a breath.

"Whoa, slow down," laughs Dodge. "My brother is covering the bill for the servers. Their wages won't be coming out of our budget."

"Oh, Dodge! That's so kind. Did everything work out with him?"

Dodge looks thoughtful for a moment. "Yes," he says finally. "It's something I should have done a long time ago."

I smile, grab his hand, and squeeze it. I look around the room. There are a lot of people here, and it seems like there's a lot of interest in the silent auction. We also have a donation box prominently placed in the center of the room with pictures of Maya and her puppies. I watch people throw money into it. Dodge has done a good job bringing his rich friends to the gala.

"This is so great," whispers Jenn. "I think we've raised some money here. Or, at least, I hope so."

The rest of the night goes smoothly and, by the end of it, we are exhausted but hopeful.

"We'll count the money tomorrow," says Jenn. "I sure hope we did it!"

The next day, we nervously add up the money. The silent auction did better than we expected, and a lot of people donated.

"Add it all up!" exclaims Jenn.

I tally it all and let out a whoop of joy. "We did it! We made forty thousand, five hundred, and eighty-nine dollars!"

I stand and jump up and down. Jenn and Cole hug and jump. Dodge cheers and does a little jig with Brad. We all cheer and high-five. Even Oscar, Sam, and Chloe bounce around barking and wagging their tails.

"I have to go," I say. "Stanley starts training today."

"Finally," says Dodge laughing.

Dodge follows me out into the parking lot. "Hey, Sarah. Good job. You did such a great job. And guess what?"

I smile at him. "What?"

"I've decided I'm going to adopt Maya and at least one of her puppies."

"Oh, wow! And now they're all going to be okay! And so is the Rescue Center."

"It sure is. We did it." Dodge gives me a hug. His strong arms wrap around me easily. They feel natural, as though they're meant to be there. I look up into his shining blue eyes and smile.

"We sure did," I whisper.

Dodge's mouth touches down on mine, and time stands still.

EPILOGUE – SIX MONTHS LATER

"Stanley!" I shout. "Stop. You've been in obedience school for longer than any other puppy I know, and, still, you misbehave."

"What did he do this time?" Dodge pops his head around the corner.

"He ate my sandwich. Again!" I laugh. "I have to make my lunch for tomorrow again now."

Dodge walks into the kitchen and gives me a peck on the cheek. "Let's go to bed. I'll make you one in the morning. We have a big week ahead of us at the Center."

I smile at Dodge, and we walk hand in hand to the bedroom. Stanley trails along behind us, his tongue lolling out of his mouth comically. We get to the bedroom, and Dodge laughs.

"We need a bigger bed," Dodge informs me. Maya and Clark are sitting on the bed looking at us. Dodge moves her gently down to the end of the bed. Clark rolls onto his back and sticks his legs in the air. Dodge tries to lift him, but he rolls around avoiding his grasp.

"Clark! I need a place to sleep also!" laughs Dodge. He finally gets a hold of Clark and moves him to the end of the bed. Just as he is about to get in, Stanley jumps up and lays his head on Dodge's pillow. His big body takes up the entire side.

EPILOGUE – SIX MONTHS LATER

"Stanley! You have a bed! It's right beside us!"

"We have a king-size bed. How much bigger can we go?" I say.

"I don't know," laughs Dodge.

He crawls into bed and smiles at me. "The best decision I made was to start volunteering at the Rescue. Thank you. Thanks for being part of my life and for helping me find myself again. I am forever grateful. I love you." Dodge strokes my hair and rests his head next to mine.

"I never thought I'd love again. And I was fine with it. And yet, I would never want to change a single thing about this. Thank you," I say. Dodge wraps his arms around me. They feel strong and safe.

"And I'm so glad that you became my marketing manager," says Dodge. "This has been the best six months financially for my business in a long time. Maybe ever. Thank you! I don't know that I can ever repay you."

"You've repaid me enough," I say. "I mean, first of all, you actually pay me." We both laugh.

"You're such a dork," he laughs. He kisses the tip of my nose.

"Takes one to know one," I say. I punch his arm lightly. Stanley snorts at me in response.

"Stanley agrees," laughs Dodge. "And that hurt! You've been working out!"

"It's all the dog walking. Stanley pulls a lot!" I say over my laughter.

Dodge snuggles into me. I never imagined my life would be so good after Doug. I never imagined that moving to this sleepy little town would be the start of such an amazing and full life. I sigh happily. I glance down at Maya and Clark at the foot of the bed. Maya licks her son as they curl up together. I watch them in the dark and smile. Our family might be unconventional, but it's ours, and we are happy.

"She is so funny with her pup," laughs Dodge. "I wonder if we'll ever fall asleep again to something other than the noises of a dog's tongue, or if we'll ever sleep not squished together because of a four-legged bed hog?"

EPILOGUE – SIX MONTHS LATER

"Do we want to fall asleep without those things?" I ask.

"No," says Dodge. "Just like I never want to fall asleep without you again."

"Ditto," I whisper, and I curl deeper into his arms.

We fall asleep like that to the sound of Stanley snoring.

THE PERFECT MOMENT OF THE HEART

CHAPTER 1

"Mickey!" I shout. "Come back!" I hightail it across the dog park toward my wayward poodle. He stands still, waiting for me to get to him. Just as I am about to grab his collar, he bounds off again. I groan and follow. I swear he smiles at me before he sprints away.

"I thought poodles were easy to train, Mickey," I grumble. "Look at your sister. You both went to obedience school!" Minnie sits quietly in the middle of the park chewing her toy.

"Looks like that one is a real handful!" a friendly voice says. I turn around and glance in the direction the voice is coming from. Standing by the edge of the park is a man I've seen here once before. He is tall, with blond hair, and he's well-dressed. He's overdressed really, to be standing in an off-leash dog park.

"Yeah, he sure is! And this is after obedience school. Imagine before!" I laugh. I brush my hair back from my face before wandering over to the man.

"I'm Ben," the man says. He smiles at me as he extends his hand. I stop and take him in. His teeth are white and straight. He is slim and fit, and he's dressed in jeans and a button-down shirt with a blazer. None of it is cheap. I should know. The blazer itself is over one thousand dollars. I sell several of them a month in my upscale boutique. In fact, this one looks like one of mine. I'm sure I've seen this man somewhere other than the dog park.

"Marissa," I say and shake his hand firmly. "Nice blazer by the way."

Ben looks down and grins. "I got it at a boutique on Second Avenue. I forgot the name."

"The Perfect Moment?" I ask.

"Yeah," Ben says. He snaps his fingers in excitement. "Great boutique. My ex-girlfriend was a regular there, and she turned me on to it."

I laugh. Should I tell him now or later that I am the owner? I decide to hold off.

"It looks great on you. Your ex had good taste," I say and wink.

"She did," Ben agrees. "Clothing-wise anyway."

I nod and smile, unsure what to say next.

This is why I'm still single. I haven't dated since my ex-husband and I split up five years ago. He was insanely jealous of my success. I've gone on two haphazard dates since then. One ended with the guy complaining about the price of the meal. When I offered to pay, he got weird and hostile. The second one spent the entire time lamenting about how much money he needed to start another business. It felt like he was trying to secure a loan from me, not date me. To say my track record for dating is poor is a grand understatement.

"This is Abe, by the way," Ben says. I look down at the large Saint Bernard sitting by his feet. "He's a bit of a shy guy. Also pretty hyper when he gets going. He's like that weird anti-social guy that runs around the playground alone for no reason."

I laugh. "I understand that behavior. I might be a little like that," I say awkwardly. Why am I so professional and successful in my work life but so awkward with men? I flush and pretend to bend down to fix my shoe.

"Uh, I think Mickey might be running again," Ben says.

I stand and look around. Mickey is gone.

"Oh, man!" I grumble and jog across the park calling his name.

Finally, I find him in some bushes. He has burrs stuck all over him. He looks up at me sheepishly and hangs his head.

"Mickey, come. It's time to go home," I say shortly. I gently attach his leash and walk him to where his sister is sitting. I fasten her leash and walk toward the entrance. Ben is chatting amicably with a pretty brunette girl when I leave. I smile and wave. He waves back and gestures for me to come over.

"I have to go to work," I call out as I leave. I can't handle another rejection right now.

CHAPTER 2

"Hey, Jenn," I say as the boutique door chimes. My friend Jenn walks in. She is wearing her usual jeans and t-shirt. Her jeans have traces of dirt on them. Such is the life of a dog rescue manager.

"How are things?" she asks as she glances around the store. It's quiet today but most Tuesdays are. The weather is just on the edge of breaking into spring and, once that happens, this entire area will become a walking haven. Traffic always picks up around that time.

"Good, overall," I say noncommittally. The boutique is doing well. I, on the other hand, am tired. I'm tired of the grind, and I'm tired of well-meaning friends trying to set me up or invite me out. Winter always burns me out, even with the three short vacations I take each year.

"How was New Years'?" Jenn asks. "We missed you this year. Also, I can't believe I haven't seen you since December. Where have you been?"

"I know, I just didn't feel like being in a crowd. I wanted some time alone. Plus, Mickey and Minnie weren't trained yet. Leaving them alone could have been an issue," I say. Mickey can be an issue even when he isn't alone. But he is such a cuddle bug, so I tolerate the behavioral challenges.

"Cole and I have a fenced backyard. You could have brought them. We know all about them, remember?" Jenn laughs. "But I get it. We all need down-time."

I nod and smile. "I hope you guys had fun though. Once the weather is warmer, I'll be around. Don't worry."

"It was fun. By the way, have you ever tried any dating apps? The reason I ask is that my sister is considering it. I've never done it." Jenn shifts nervously. I can tell she is prying just a little. All my friends want me to date more. The truth is, I'd like to, but I just never meet anyone that seems to be compatible with me.

"No, I feel like I'm too old for that." I laugh, but it falls flat.

"You're thirty-five, Marissa." Jenn laughs.

I grin. She's right. The truth is that I'm just scared to try it. I've heard so many horror stories.

"I met a guy at the dog park yesterday. Ben. Seems nice," I say.

"Uh-huh, and is he calling you, or are you calling him?" Jenn interjects.

"No, but I am meeting him at the dog park after work," I say quickly.

Jenn smiles, obviously pleased. "Great! Let me know how it goes."

"I will! There's just one thing about Ben..." I say tentatively.

"What's that"

"He shopped here with his ex," I say.

"So? Do you remember her?"

"I'm not sure. Maybe. I probably have her information in my file, if she was a regular customer."

"Do you know her name?"

"No, but he looks familiar to me."

"By the way, those Louboutin shoes you got last week, any chance you have a size seven? I'll have to make quite a few payments, but I'd love to own a pair of those just once in my life," Jenn says and grins. "Obviously, they're not for work."

"Yep. Let me put them aside for you," I say.

"Great! See you soon!" Jenn bounds out the door as quickly as she came in. I laugh and shake my head. I might not have a significant other, but my friends are out-of-this-world amazing.

I close the boutique early and head to the dog park. I am hoping to see Ben, even though I tell myself it's just for Mickey and Minnie.

Ben is at the park with Abe when I arrive. Abe runs around the perimeter of the park in circles while Ben sits and sips a coffee on the bench.

"Hi!" I say brightly. Looking into his blue eyes, I feel butterflies dance around inside me. Calm down Marissa, I coach myself. You are literally jumping the gun here. He was with another woman here at the park, remember? She may have been his girlfriend.

Ben's face lights up when he sees me. "Hey, Marissa, how are you?" he asks. He scratches Mickey behind the ears. The big dog wags his tail in excitement.

"I'm great," I say. I unleash both dogs and glance at Ben. He stares at me intently.

"I wanted to introduce you to my sister the other day," he says.

"Your sister?" I ask.

"Yeah, the girl I was chatting with? She lives just down the street, and she owns the dog grooming store by the park entrance," Ben says as he smiles.

"Oh, wow!" I say. I feel stupid now after assuming he was flirting with her.

"Yeah, I thought you might like to meet her. She gives discounts to some of the patrons she has who hang out here," Ben says.

"I'd love to next time," I say, still feeling foolish.

We both stare at each other awkwardly for a second before turning to the dogs.

"Where's Mickey?" I ask.

Ben glances around the park and shakes his head. "I don't see him."

I take off across the park. Ben jogs along beside me. I spot Mickey a second later in a bush. He bounds out and greets me excitedly.

"Mickey!" I yell. "What the heck, dude?"

In response, Mickey jumps on me and knocks me into the mud. I land with a splat and a groan.

Ben laughs and extends his hand. I take it shyly, and he pulls me up.

"He even went to obedience school," I grumble. I stare at my jacket in dismay. It is covered in mud.

"Well, that was money well spent," quips Ben. I glance at him, angry at myself and humiliated. My anger melts when I see Ben's grin. He winks at me and scratches Mickey behind the ears.

We walk back to where Minnie and Abe are waiting. Both dogs look at us expectantly.

"Looks like somebody wants treats," Ben says as he laughs. He pulls a handful of beef jerky treats out of his pocket. Before I can tell him not to, he gives both Minnie and Mickey a treat.

I groan inwardly. Minnie will have diarrhea for sure now. Her stomach is so sensitive.

"Is something wrong?" Ben asks.

"She has a bad stomach. She only eats all-natural or dried foods as treats," I say. My voice sounds clipped even to my own ears.

"I'm sorry," says Ben. He looks genuinely upset about his blunder.

"It's okay," I mumble. Why am I being such a nincompoop to this guy? He didn't know. Still, isn't it proper to ask someone before feeding their dog? I am tired and covered in mud. All I want to do is go home.

"Well, it was nice seeing you again anyway," says Ben. "I hope Minnie is okay. I should have asked. Here's my number in case anything happens. It's all my fault." He pulls out a card and hands it to me.

"Thanks," I say as I stick it in my pocket. I consider telling him I can afford the vet bill if something does happen, but I remain silent.

He is just trying to be nice, I think to myself as I leash both dogs and load them into the car.

CHAPTER 3

My assistant, Paula, echoes my thoughts the next day. "Sounds like he was just trying to be nice, however misguided it might have been."

"Yeah, you're right. I don't know why I'm being so judgy," I agree.

"You said he's nice. Why not ask him out for coffee or a dog play-date?" Paula reorganizes racks as she talks. She moves swiftly and with purpose.

"I guess I could. I don't know. I feel so weird about it all. I haven't dated in so long I almost forget how." I cringe as I speak. It really has been a long time since I've even been on a date, much less been involved with someone.

The last person was Mike, my husband, and that ended abruptly one Sunday afternoon when he packed and moved out of my house after declaring his undying love for my previous assistant. Last I heard, they were trying for baby number two. Baby number one was born seven months after he left me.

"Marissa!" Paula turns and faces me, several jackets poised in mid-air. "Listen to yourself. You know you want to date again so why not take the leap? Just ask. Don't put any expectations on it. Maybe he'll say yes, or maybe he'll say no. But you won't ever date again if you don't put yourself out there."

I nod silently. She's right. My life is amazing, and it would be wonderful to share it with someone.

"I know it's scary," says Paula. She shifts the rack in front of her as she speaks. "But so was adopting two dogs. And so was opening this boutique. And so on. My point is, you're a badass. So go ahead, and just do it. I believe in you. And who knows? He might be as great as he is great-looking."

I sigh. Paula is right, and she knows me well. I will avoid this at all costs even though I'd love to share my life with someone. Why am I making this so complicated, anyway?

"Okay, fine. I will. Next time I see him," I say.

Paula changes price tags carefully as she speaks. "You have his number. Just call him."

Damn. Why did I have to tell her that part?

"Okay, fine. After lunch I will," I agree.

Lunch comes and goes. I busy myself with ordering new products and with checking our second-quarter sales. Ben crosses my mind several times, but I make no move to call.

I have a business to run, after all. I don't have time to make idle conversation when there's work to be done.

"Did you call him yet?" Paula asks as she pops her head into my office. I shake my head.

"No, I'm just finishing the ordering. How do you feel about culottes? Some design houses are doing them this season, but between you, me, and the lamppost, I think they're kind of cheesy."

"Agreed," Paula says and laughs. "By the way, did you happen to see that the shelter is doing another fundraiser and adoption event?"

"What I don't need is another stubborn dog." I laugh.

"I brought it up because we agreed to sponsor it, remember? We said we would at the last event. And I agree that, unless you hire an assistant for me, we can't do another four-legged family member," Paula says. We both laugh. On days that I'm busy with work, Paula takes Mickey and Minnie out for me. Mickey behaves even worse for her than he does for me. It's a good thing she has a sense of humor with that guy. You really have to.

"Right, of course. I remember. It just seems like this year is racing by, you know? I can't believe the spring fundraiser is here already! We decided to sell designer dog attire at it, correct? Have we ordered it yet? Are we on track?" I rattle off a list of items that need to be attended to before the event.

Paula faces me and grins. "It's all ordered. We're doing several brands. Burberry and Versace, of course. And Chanel, as well as Chloe, and several other lines have dog jackets in their fall collection. It's going to be a lot of fun."

"Wow! Thanks, Paula. I don't know what I would do without you!" I'm excited thinking about it. I love jackets and booties for my four-legged friends. Minnie and Mickey have matching jackets and boots.

"You'd have a lot less time to deal with the delinquent adolescent that is Mickey!" She grins at me as she says it.

"True story," I say. I busy myself with ordering the summer stock for the store. Paula whistles as she works. Both dogs sleep in the corner at my feet. My life is pretty amazing, I think to myself. Even without a significant other to share it with.

That evening, I head home to change before loading Minnie and Mickey in my SUV and heading to the park. Ben is standing in the park chatting with his sister when I arrive.

"Marissa, this is Tammy. Tammy, Marissa," Ben says by way of hello.

"Hi, Tammy, it's nice to meet you."

We stand awkwardly for a moment.

"Ben tells me you own the grooming place down the street?"

"Yep, sure do. What do you do?" Tammy pets her Rottweiler absentmindedly as we chat. He leans into her with a look of pure bliss on his massive face.

"I, uh, I own a clothing boutique uptown," I say. I glance at Ben. I didn't tell him it was the one his ex-girlfriend frequented. I feel foolish for not saying something then. I don't know why I didn't.

Just because Mike was intimidated by my success, doesn't mean every man is.

"That's amazing," says Tammy. "Which one?"

I sigh inwardly. Why is that always the first question people ask? I'm suddenly shy. I glance at Ben, and he stares at me intently. I can't read his expression.

"Oh, just a small boutique near the strip," I reply vaguely.

Why did I hedge on the specifics, yet again? I want to be liked for me, not for my success.

"Tell me more about your grooming shop," I say, changing the subject.

"I started it four years ago with my ex. I bought him out when we split up a year ago. The best thing that ever happened to me, to be honest," Tammy says. "That man wanted me to have a cute little store but, when I started making more than him, he split."

"I can relate to that," I say and laugh.

"Mickey took off again," Ben says suddenly. I glance at the edge of the dog park. He is bounding across it into the bushes and forested area.

"Shoot! Be right back," I say. Ben takes off beside me. His long legs move quickly. He pulls ahead of me at a fast jog.

"Mickey!" I shout. I can see him chasing something. It isn't until Ben is almost on top of him that I realize it's a skunk.

"Oh, crap! Ben! He's chasing a skunk..."

Ben screams suddenly as the animal unleashes a mist of putrid spray all over him and Mickey.

"Oh, my gosh!" I shout. Ben looks stunned for a second, his eyes watering. Stumbling, he moves away from the bushes and toward me.

"I can't see," he wails. "Damn skunk! It burns!"

I stop abruptly in front of Ben and carefully guide him toward the water station. Mickey lies on the ground and whimpers, pawing his eyes incessantly.

"Here," I say gently. "Let's rinse your eyes."

The water is cold and unpleasant, but Ben sits solemnly as I wash his eyes out.

"This jacket will never be the same," he groans as I accidentally dump water on it.

"I'll get you a new one," I say. "It's covered in skunk anyway. It'll never come clean now."

"You don't need to replace it," he sighs. His face and shoulders slump in defeat.

"I can, and I will. Not sure if I can get the exact same one again. It's from two seasons ago, but I know the new season has something similar. I'm so sorry. If not for my degenerate dog, none of this would have happened." I glare at Mickey for a second. He whimpers and lays down, his tongue lolling out of his mouth.

"Come here, Mickey," I say. "You need water."

"How do I get the smell off my skin?" asks Ben.

Tammy approaches cautiously. "You need hydrogen peroxide, baking soda, and dish soap," she affirms. "I sell a product that works also, but I'm not sure if I have any in stock. But I guarantee those three things mixed together will work. Equal parts in the tub diluted by half with water. It literally got it all off my daughter's skin when Kenny got sprayed when she was walking him."

Ben moans. "I don't even have a bathtub at my condo. Shower only. What a stupid decision that was!"

I laugh, and then I clamp my hand over my mouth. "Sorry. That's a bit amusing though. Joking aside, come to my place. I have a massive soaker tub for me. And these guys."

Ben shifts around, obviously uncomfortable. "Oh, gosh. Awkward!" he exclaims. Tammy giggles.

"What choice do you have?" she asks. "My tub is way too small for you to fit well."

Ben nods, and he looks miserable.

"Right, then," I say. "Everybody, get in my SUV. I'll pop into the pharmacy and grab the supplies. You guys wait in the car. We'll get this sorted. I promise!"

Ben nods. I quickly leash Mickey and Minnie. Abe follows us obediently off-leash. We all pile into the car and head to the pharmacy. Between Ben and Mickey, the smell in the car is almost unbearable. I buy all the peroxide and baking soda they have and most of the dish soap. The cashier looks at me quizzically as she rings me up.

"Skunk situation," I say, aware that my clothing probably also reeks of the offending scent.

The cashier nods and offers a tight-lipped smile. "I figured as much." Her response is clipped. I glance around, and everyone is staring at me. Yep, I must smell as bad as Ben does.

"Sorry, all," I say and smile brightly. "My dog is a challenge."

I quickly rush out to the car and drive to my place. I feel weird knowing I'm going to have to let Ben come in, but what choice do I have? My condo is a large three-bedroom affair with an open concept and views from every room. I have a hot tub on the terrace and massive twelve-foot ceilings. I bought this place after my store was written up in both *The Times* and in *Woman's Weekly*. I have some notoriety around these parts. I've done just enough publicity to make sure business is booming and little enough that most people have no idea who I am. I like leading a simple life with my dogs. Sometimes, though, I do wish that I had someone to share it with.

For several years, I had been convinced Mike was that person. In the beginning, he was attentive and loving. He helped me out when my boutique first started. His helpfulness turned to disinterest and finally silent anger as my business grew. Financially, it was a hit to me. Emotionally, it had destroyed me for a period.

I force myself back to the present. I park in the underground garage and hurry around to get the dogs and Ben out of the car. Ben's face is red and blotchy, his eyes swollen but not shut.

"Wow, you live here?" Ben says. The admiration in his voice makes me blush.

"Yes," I say. "I bought it a few years ago before prices skyrocketed."

"Nice!"

"I love it here. Close to walking trails, hiking paths, and the water. It really has a bit of everything. The commute to work can be daunting, though, especially on long weekends." I guide the dogs and Ben into the elevator hoping that the doorman doesn't see, or smell, us.

We ride the elevator in silence as I mentally prepare myself for the massive undertaking that is coming next. My eyes are watering badly by the time we get to my floor both because of the putrid smell and the enclosed space.

"Okay, here we are," I wheeze and open the condo door.

I quickly lead everyone to the washroom and fill the massive tub with the odor-fighting concoction. Then I turn and look at Ben expectantly.

"What? You just want me to drop trou right here?" he jokes. I look around the room.

"Well, no. I can leave, but I want the dogs in here with you. I don't want this horrific smell all over my furniture," I say.

"Okay. Well, the tub is big enough for Mickey and me. Is Minnie okay? She was next to Mickey the whole way home," Ben says. His fingers tremble slightly as he undoes his shirt buttons. "Man, the smell of this is making me feel ill."

"I'm so sorry this happened," I say. I genuinely mean it. I feel terrible for Ben and Mickey.

I sniff Minnie critically. She does stink but not as badly as Mickey or Ben. Abe smells like the trees, with no trace of skunk on him at all. I let Abe out into the living room.

"Okay, so I'll leave Minnie tied up here. I'll wash me and her when you and Mickey are done." I look at Ben and wait.

"Uh, I can get Mickey in the tub with me. You can go if you want," he says awkwardly. He pulls his shirt off. I stare at his muscular chest with admiration for a second before I catch myself. I flush deep crimson and force myself to concentrate.

"Sure. Once your clothes are off, toss them out the door. I'll run to the boutique and grab you something similar. So just hang out in the tub until I'm back. Traffic should be okay right now but if it's slow, just keep soaking." I feel better once I have a game plan, a solution. "I'll leave the rest of the supplies here in case you need to mix another tub."

Ben nods and undoes his pants. I turn abruptly and leave.

I change my clothes and hurry out the door. I call Paula from the car.

"So, he's naked in your tub right now?" she asks, laughing.

"He sure is. I'm headed to you to get clothes for him. He has a

Burberry blazer from two years ago and a Dolce pair of fitted slacks. They're the lower-end ones, but we can give him the expensive blue pair we just got. Size thirty-four. They won't need to be hemmed. He's tall. I'm also going to need Calvin boxers and socks. We might have some in the back. I did sell them for a while. If not, I'll run to Saks and grab those." I mentally picture Ben's chest and grin.

"And a shirt?" Paula asks. "Or is he so hot we're making him go shirtless?"

I laugh. "No, I mean I'd like to. But no. His shirt is mid-expense so just find him something that matches the pants and blazer. His shoes will have to do. I'll just give him cash to replace those."

"Dish soap and baking soda will take it out of canvas shoes," says Paula. "Marly got sprayed a couple of years ago, and I had to wash everything including my shoes after he rolled on them. Also, do you want to take him some track pants and a shirt for lounging? In case he isn't fully unscented when you get back?"

"Thanks! And, yes, good call" I say. Paula has been a breath of fresh air since I hired her. She's one of my best friends and absolutely indispensable to my business.

When I get to the store, Paula has everything laid out on the counter, including socks and underwear.

"Perfect!" I say and hug her. She laughs and wrinkles her nose.

"Do I still stink?" I ask.

"Nah, I'm just teasing," she says and grins. "Don't worry about coming back today. I've got the store and payroll. Also, I couriered some of the dog jackets here for the fundraiser. The rest will arrive later in the week. Once you're back at work, you can look over the budget and invoices again before I reconcile. Sounds good?"

"Amazing," I say. "I would never be able to do half the stuff I do without you!"

"I know, girl. That's why you pay me so well!" Paula hugs me again. "By the way, all the dog coat designers offer matching jackets for their human counterparts. We should consider having a catalog at the event and allowing people to order their jackets to match their dogs'. You know that'll be a big hit with the purse-dog crowd."

"Agreed! I'll leave it to you," I say.

"Go! And invite him to stay for dinner!" Paula pushes me playfully toward the door.

I zip Ben's new clothes into a wardrobe bag and hurry back to my condo.

Ben is still in the tub when I get back.

This is so awkward, I think for the fiftieth time as I walk to the washroom.

"Hey, how's it going?" I say through the door.

"Pretty good. I think the smell is almost gone," Ben says. "This stuff works well."

"I have clothes for you," I say. "Can I come and put them in there?"

"Yeah. The bubbles from the dish soap are basically a blanket," laughs Ben. "Come in."

I take a deep breath and enter the spacious bathroom. Ben sits in the tub with Mickey. The smell in the bathroom has lessened, but it is not completely gone.

"Smells a lot better," I say. I lean over to sniff Mickey, careful to divert my eyes from Ben.

"What's the matter? Never seen a grown man bathe with a dog before?" Ben asks, and he laughs deeply. His eyes dance in amusement, and his straight white teeth light up his face. "Seriously, though. This is awkward as hell and, although I am deeply appreciative of your help, I kind of also want to crawl into a hole and die of embarrassment."

"Why?" I ask. "It was my silly dog's fault that you're in this predicament."

"True. But bathing at some strange woman's house is not my usual way of meeting people," says Ben. He laughs again and his eyes lock with mine. I feel my stomach dance with excitement.

"I, uh, brought you some clothes," I stammer. "I tossed the old ones and brought some new." I hold up my selections and smile shyly.

"Thanks. You have great taste. Where did you get it all?" he asks. "I should pay for it."

"No need. It was my fault. All of it," I say.

"It must have cost you a fortune," Ben says. "My ex had expensive taste and, honestly, most of my wardrobe she picked out. It's nice to own something she didn't buy for a change since we've been apart for so long. I just kind of hate shopping for myself, so I haven't." Ben pauses and looks at me. "Sorry, am I rambling? I'm just noticing my bubbles are popping at an alarming rate."

I laugh and hurry to the door. "Okay, get dressed. Here's a towel. Leave Mickey in the tub. I'll deal with him in a second. He loves it there, anyway."

I exit and close the door. I can hear Ben shuffling around in the bathroom. He emerges in the tracksuit.

"Love it!" I say. I genuinely mean it. It fits him well, hugging all the right places. Ben looks sporty and stylish.

"Thanks. I do too. At least let me pay for this," he says.

"It's not the biggest deal," I say. "You can but, honestly, I bought it as a gift and as a way of saying sorry."

"Well, in that case, let me take you to dinner as a thank you for the thank you." Ben grins.

I nod and smile. "Yeah, I'd like that."

I wash Minnie and myself. By the time I'm done, the smell of skunk is mostly a distant memory.

After we stop and get shoes for Ben, he takes me to an elegant French restaurant located on the upper floor of the prominent Ritz-Carlton. Its cozy, dark brown leather booths and quaint, dim lighting make it a perfect place for relaxing after a long day at work and on intimate dates alike.

We sit in a quiet booth in the corner, away from the dark brown circular craft cocktail bar. Ben orders a seafood tower for us to start, and we hungrily tuck into oysters, mussels, and crabs.

"So, tell me more about your store," Ben says between bites of delectable seafood.

"It's not that exciting," I say as I carefully pull a long section of crab meat from the shell. "I started it because I wanted to do something different. I wanted to showcase designers but not always the classic styles that the department stores did. I wanted to be unique. I guess I have accomplished that."

Ben nods. "I'd love to see it, sometime."

I smile at him.

You already have, I think to myself. I don't know why I don't tell him that I own his ex's beloved boutique. Part of me wants to remain anonymous, I guess. Another part of me wants to make sure he isn't intimidated by my obvious success.

Real men aren't intimidated, I remind myself. Better to just tell him now.

"How did you end up adopting Abe?" I ask brightly.

"I saw him at the last adoption event and had to have him. He's just so funny," Ben says. I smile.

"He sure is a big galoot," I say and laugh. "How did you train him? I remember him being a bit wild at the adoption event."

"You were there?" Ben asks. He puts his fork down and looks at me.

"Yeah. My boutique sponsored it," I say tentatively.

"Oh," says Ben, looking confused.

"I mean we were one of many sponsors," I say hastily. This was sort of true. We were one of three sponsors.

"Cool. Yeah, well, I did take him to obedience school, but he was the same sort of pupil that Mickey was. Bad. So finally, I hired a private trainer. Needless to say, it was not a cheap or easy solution. I can recommend him to you if you want to do more work with Mickey," Ben says.

I nod and laugh. "I suppose he needs it."

Ben laughs, and I feel myself flush red. I'm glad he has a sense of humor. At least he isn't mad at me for the whole skunk thing.

"It was a pretty great experience," Ben says. "This guy is good. He knows what he is doing, for sure."

"Okay, I guess it's worth a try," I say.

Our dinners arrive. I admire the beauty of the plating of my filet mignon and vegetables.

"This is lovely," I say. "Thank you."

"No, thank you. It's been a long time since I've been out for dinner. Even if it is all because of a skunk mishap." Ben smiles wryly at me. His blue eyes penetrate deeply into me. I feel oddly vulnerable, something I am not used to.

"I'm so sorry again for that," I stammer.

"It's fine," laughs Ben. "I was just teasing." He pats my hand with his and leaves his sitting on top of mine. I feel oddly nervous and exhilarated by his touch.

Stop it, I chide myself. You don't need to be getting all schoolgirl giddy about this. He might just be friendly.

"Tell me more about your business," I say.

"I work in real estate," he says. "I redevelop buildings. You know a lot of the buildings down by the midtown shopping area?" I nod. That's where The Perfect Moment is located. I know it well.

"Well, between you, me, and the lamppost, a lot of that area is going to be torn down and redeveloped in the next few years," Ben says matter-of-factly. "It's unfortunate. I suspect that means a lot of the old businesses will be moved."

I pause and feel a moment of panic. "Really? Like what buildings?"

Ben lists a bunch. None of them are the building I am located in but the ones he mentions are alarmingly close to mine.

"What about the owners? How does that work?" I ask. I vaguely wonder if I can afford to buy the building my store is in. It might be a good investment, anyway.

"Well, if they're private, the owner has to be bought out. Or the building remains," Ben replies. "Why? Do you own real estate down there?"

"No, I was just curious," I say. I feel oddly deflated by his information as if he is somehow to blame for the redevelopment.

"I think everyone will sell, though. Some of them are even looking to do it now," Ben says.

"Do you think 5454 Broadway will sell? The building where that boutique your ex liked is?" I ask, my face neutral.

"Probably," he nods. "I think it's in phase two, but I could be wrong."

I make a mental note to google it when I get home. I make a second mental note to call the management company and find out the owners' information. It would be terrible to have to close my boutique. The cost of renting real estate right now is astronomical. There's no way I'd be able to afford my lease as easily at today's prices. Maybe it's time to move the entire shop online like Paula suggested last year when sales were down.

"You okay?" Ben asks. "You got quiet all of a sudden. Did I say something wrong?"

"No, it's all good," I say. "I love that area though," I finish lamely. Why am I not telling him the truth?

I have to tell him about the boutique. How weird would it be if I did know his ex?

Ben and I wander around the park after dinner. His hand lightly rests in mine. It's a warm evening, comfortable for an evening walk. The air smells fresh and clean. I smile to myself and steal a glance at Ben. He is smiling slightly as we walk. His handsome face is relaxed, and he is fully present. I feel a surge of affection pass through me. I know I'm being unreasonable about his view of successful women, but now it's been a few days, and it just seems so much more awkward to tell him.

"What's your plan for tomorrow?" he asks as we stop in front of a cherry blossom tree.

"Work," I say tentatively. "My store is sponsoring the rescue fundraiser."

"That's amazing. What a great cause! I'm going to be there to help the rescue as well." Ben turns his head and smiles at me. Our eyes lock, and I can't look away. His blue eyes penetrate me, and he moves closer. I lean into him, and our lips touch. Electricity courses through me when I feel his soft, masculine lips on mine. Our kiss deepens, and I relax into his embrace. His strong arms hold me, and I rest my head on his chest.

"I have something to tell you," I say suddenly.

"Sure." Ben's eyes meet mine, and he waits.

I stare intently at his thick hair and beautiful eyes. The dusk air hangs around us wrapping us in warmth.

"I wasn't fully honest about the store I own," I start.

Ben raises one eyebrow and nods, encouraging me to go on.

"I own The Perfect Moment." The words spill out of my mouth quickly before I can change my mind.

"I love that place," Ben says.

"I know. I didn't want to tell you because my ex was so intimidated by my success, and I like you. I was scared you would be the same. I know it's silly now, but after not telling you at our first meeting, it was hard to backpedal. I'm sorry."

Ben pauses a moment and then laughs heartily. "Sorry for what? Did you honestly think I'd not want to hang out with you because you're successful?"

"It happens more than you'd think," I say. Relief floods me, and I smile.

"I'm sure it does but that's not me," he says.

"I know it seems so silly now that I've said it out loud."

"We all have our fears and insecurities. I mean, without this, you'd be perfect." Ben grins at me.

"I guess..."

"I'm totally joking. No one's perfect. But you are beautiful and successful, so I guess you have to have something..." Ben gently runs his finger down my cheek.

"We should get back to the dogs," I say reluctantly. I want this moment to last forever.

Ben nods, and we stroll back to the car.

Mickey and Minnie are asleep when we arrive at my condo. Abe waits by the door patiently. He eyeballs me quizzically as we enter.

"I think someone needs to go out," Ben says.

"I'll get these two. We can go together," I suggest. I bend down tentatively and smell Mickey. He smells faintly of skunk still, but the majority of it is gone.

"Thank goodness your sister told us what to do!" I laugh after I say it.

"No kidding. Eau de Skunk is not the scent I'm going for at work tomorrow."

CHAPTER 4

Paula races around the store like a frantic ball of energy. My laptop is open in front of me. I stare at the spreadsheet trying to concentrate. The fundraiser is in two days, and there is still a lot to be done.

"So, what's the story with Ben?" she asks as she sorts and moves inventory.

"He kissed me. It was nice. I like him," I say.

"Did you ever find out who his ex is?" she asks.

"No. I don't care," I say. I know that I could check our client profiles to see who bought the blazer he was in, but I don't have any reason to do that. Let sleeping dogs lie, as the saying goes.

"The doggie jackets haven't arrived from Chanel yet?" asks Paula.

I frown. "They should have arrived this week. We better find out where they are. Those are the ones that are going to make or break the money we're able to donate!"

Paula nods and gets on the phone. Her fingers move quickly.

What would I do without her?

Paula listens intently to the saleslady. "Is there any way we can come get them?"

She nods silently and chews her lip. This can't be good. The only time Paula chews her lip is if she is upset.

"They got stopped at a weigh station. They're on their way, but they might not make it. She said we can drive to the storage warehouse and pick up an order and then just return the shipped ones when they arrive." Paula looks nervous as she speaks. Nervousness is not something Paula feels often.

"Shoot! Okay, how far away is that?" I wring my hands and mentally take inventory of the dog jackets we do have. We might have enough, but the donation won't make the impact both of us truly want to make.

"It's like two hours almost," Paula says slowly.

"Damn. Okay, well, what do we do?" I ask.

The front door chimes and I glance at the customer. My eyes widen when I realize it's Ben. Abe is sitting outside waiting for him.

"Hey! I just wanted to stop by and see if the dogs wanted to come to the park with me? I figured you were busy working," Ben says. "What's wrong?" He looks at Paula and me, and he takes in our expressions of sadness.

"The dog jackets we ordered for the fundraiser got stuck on the way and are going to be late," I tell him. "We could drive there but it's around two hours away. And the dog rescue fundraiser is in two days. So basically, we have tomorrow to drive there, get the stock, drive back, and get everything else ready. I'm not sure that the two of us can do it."

"We have to try," Paula says with determination. She grins. "I refuse to give up without a fight."

"I admire your tenacity," I say to her.

Ben watches the exchange silently. His eyes crinkle in thought.

"I could drive to get the order," he says.

"What, really?" I say.

"That would be great!" says Paula quickly. "I'll let them know you're coming." She dials quickly and relays the information. "It's Ben picking them up. Ben," she puts her hand over the phone. "What's your last name?"

"Ben Drummond," he says. My brain snaps into focus. I remember him now. His ex is a prominent C-level director at some tech company. She was written about in the same magazine article I was. I feel an odd sense of relief flood over me. He really was telling me the truth.

"They're expecting you mid-afternoon tomorrow," Paula tells Ben. "Here's the address and directions. You know, in case your GPS doesn't work."

Ben nods and smiles. "Roger that. One dog-rescue-fundraiser-save coming right up."

"Thank you, Ben. Are you sure this is okay?" I ask.

"Yes, but you owe me." Ben smiles at me as he says it.

"Anything. What? Name it."

"This," Ben steps towards me. His fingers tip my head up to his. His lips touch mine, sensually and soft. His eyes penetrate me, and I shiver with a very pleasant feeling inside.

Silently, he turns and strides out the door and down the sidewalk. Abe follows him, glancing back only once as he matches Ben's pace.

"Wow," says Paula. "That was smoldering. And I didn't even get kissed."

I laugh and grip the counter behind me for support.

"Yeah, you got that right. Now let's just hope he delivers on those jackets."

The next morning, we arrive at the rescue center event early to take care of any last-minute preparations. Jenn and her marketing manager, Sarah, from the rescue center are flitting all around to help with the set-up.

"I hope he gets here." I fret as we set up our booth for the fundraiser. I stare at my phone for about the seven-hundredth time since lunch.

"He will," says Paula. "Help me with this display."

By four o'clock, the booth is ready. The two displays in front are empty, set aside for the most important items — the missing dog coats.

"They've been picked up. Gertrude just messaged me to tell me. He's going to be cutting it close getting back here, especially with traffic." Paula says this casually, but I can tell she is concerned.

My phone buzzes. A text from Ben. "Got them. On the way back. Be there before start."

"He's got this," Paula says after she reads the message. I nod and look around the rescue. All the desks have been moved out of the main space. Jenn buzzes around putting up marketing promo and fixing the aesthetics.

"This is the first fundraiser and adoption we've done here," she says. "I'm pretty nervous. Doing them at the pet store is different. Less responsibility. What if we didn't advertise enough, and it's a flop? What if I didn't advertise the sponsors enough? We basically have a doggy marketplace here. It's incredible. I hope we did enough!" She glances around nervously.

"Relax, girl," says Cole. He stands beside her and rests a hand on her shoulder. "You did more than enough. And all the vendors here had it on their social media as well. We've got this."

We all smile at him. Cole's right. We do have this. We're all good at what we do.

The next morning I'm not so sure, though. Ben has not arrived with the jackets yet. Paula quickly assesses the situation.

"Worst case, we move this display and showcase Burberry. It's not as great, but it will have to do. We can still do this. We have more booties we can put out also if we need them." I nod and prepare to move the empty display.

At ten minutes to nine, there is a line of customers waiting outside. I admit defeat and prepare to quickly move the vacant display. Ben tried; I reason to myself. I hope that he hasn't had an accident or something. I move one rack aside, ready to hide it in the back.

"He's here!" Paula says at five minutes before we're supposed to start.

"He is?" I ask. I look at the waiting customers. "Where?"

"Right here!" Ben's deep voice resonates behind me.

"Oh!" I gasp.

"I came in the back door."

Ben carries two massive boxes. I grab them from him, and Paula and I get to work. Five minutes. We've got this. Ben runs outside to grab the final box.

Jenn opens the doors just as we are putting the last few jackets out. I look around at our booth.

"Perfect!" I proclaim.

"The extra sizes are under the table here," Paula says, kicking the box gently. "We got this!"

I watch in amazement as people file into the shelter. This might turn out to be the best fundraising event they have ever had. I flush with pride, thrilled to be part of it.

Ben stands beside me beaming. I can tell by the look on his face, he is just as proud as I am.

CHAPTER 5

"We raised over thirty-thousand dollars!" Jenn tells me excitedly, ten hours later. "Do you know how many dogs we can rescue now?"

I smile when she says it. This is a huge win for the rescue and for all the vendors alike. Ben stands beside me grinning almost as much as Paula and me.

"I'm glad I got to be a part of this," he says as we pack the remaining inventory.

We've almost sold out of everything. We did better than any of us could have imagined.

"Me, too. Thank you. We couldn't have pulled it off without you," I tell him.

"Yeah, you could have. But I'm glad I could help," Ben says. He shifts his feet nervously.

"You look like someone that's about to confess to his mom that he broke the vase," Paula says as she tapes the top of a box.

"You kind of do. What gives?" I ask.

"Well," says Ben. "I wanted to wait until after this to tell you."

"Tell me what?"

"The building that your store is in is up for redevelopment."

I stop mid-packing. "What does that mean?" I ask evenly.

"At best, it means you'll have to close while they build the condos, and then you can reopen. The main floor is slated to be all retail still."

"And at worst?"

"They won't allow you to renew your lease."

I sigh and focus my efforts back on tear-down. I feel defeated despite our massive win today at the fundraiser.

"I'm sorry. I don't have a poker face," says Ben quietly. "I got the news mid-way through the fundraiser, and it was all I could do to not tell you right away."

"It's okay," says Paula brightly. "Worst case, we move. We've got this. Do you know how many dog owners are going to become regular clients? Maybe we can change our marketing focus to be more dog-centric. You'd like that more anyway." I nod silently. Paula is always the voice of optimism and reason. It's one of the many reasons I love her.

"Maybe you can even buy a small building to house the boutique," says Ben enthusiastically. "I happen to know a commercial real estate agent with inside info." He laughs.

"Thanks, guys," I say. "You're right. Everything is going to be okay."

Ben wraps his arms around me and squeezes. He smooths my hair off my face and stares deeply into my eyes.

"It's all going to be okay. I promise. Look at what the three of us accomplished today. I'm with you. Every step. I promise." Ben leans into me and kisses me lightly. "You're a strong woman, and there is nothing you can't accomplish. I know that. Let's just take it one step at a time."

I nod and stand on my tippy-toes. My lips brush his before I turn to Paula.

"I can't imagine a better team to have," I say. I really mean it. I have no idea what the future with Ben might look like, but I believe him when he says he'll help. I smile and take a deep breath. This might be the beginning of a whole new chapter for all of us.

EPILOGUE – 6 MONTHS LATER

"I can't believe how well this worked out," I say. I pivot in a full circle staring at the shiny new racks in amazement.

"It's amazing," says Paula. She stands beside me, her back straight and proud. I've made her the new general manager of our entire operation.

"It's really amazing, the work you guys have done here," Ben says. He stands beside me holding my hand. At our feet, Mickey, Minnie, and Abe sit and wait for us.

"You helped. And anyway, without you, I'd have never been able to pull this off."

"I didn't do much. You're the passion behind it."

I nod. Ben is not wrong about that. Paula and I have completely revamped the business. We're the first "dog and person" boutique. We have the clothing side, the same as I had before. We have a full dog clothing section now. High end. Designer. The same as our clothing. Burberry, Chloe, Chanel, and Gucci to name a few. Besides that, we have a full spa and doggy spa so that you and your four-legged friend can spend some time getting pampered. The spa has a sit-down restaurant with a doggy play area so you can eat while your furry counterparts play. It's monitored and state of the art. The food at the restaurant features wares from local farmers. I hired a local chef, and the menu changes daily. I have a local animal nutritionist that creates take-away meals and cookies for the dogs.

Paula is the brains behind the rebranding. It's classy, stylish, and, frankly, I am darned excited about it.

"Mickey wants to play in the doggy daycare," laughs Ben. Mickey eyeballs him patiently. He sits and wags his tail, his tongue lolling out of his mouth in a lopsided grin.

"Look how patient my big boy is now," I coo. I scratch him behind the ears and grin. "That trainer sure was worth it. What a great guy!"

"I told you! He did wonders with Abe, too." Ben circles around the space in awe. "This really is incredible."

I nod. "I can hardly wait till the grand opening party tomorrow. We've done so well since the soft opening."

"We just hit 1000 subscribers for the newsletter, and our social media has tripled in the past three days." Paula hops from one foot to the other excitedly. "We've got over one thousand people who RSVP'd for the party, although some won't come. That's always the way. But the marketing is working well. The restaurant is booked for the next few weeks and so is the spa and doggy spa. All that will translate into sales in the boutique." She pauses and thinks. "Oh, and I have local news and two magazines coming tomorrow. Maybe three. I'm just waiting to hear from *Paws and People*."

I high-five her and smile again. I can hardly believe how amazing everything is working out. The best thing that ever happened was that my lease wasn't renewed in the old building. I could not have imagined a better outcome than the one we have.

"Go home, you two. I need you both alert and on it tomorrow." Paula playfully shoos us toward the door.

"Come on, guys! Mickey! Minnie!" Both of my doggies come running. Abe saunters along behind them, alone yet part of the gang. I leash all three dogs and turn to Ben.

"Ready to go?" I ask.

"I sure am," he agrees. He pulls his blazer closed and ties his scarf around his neck.

"It's fall! It's hardly that cold." I laugh.

EPILOGUE – 6 MONTHS LATER

"You never know when a stylish scarf can make all the difference. Sometimes it's the difference between a good day and a great day. Style. That's what you taught me, isn't it?" Ben grabs my hand as we walk out the door. Paula waves goodbye and laughs.

"I mean, there are lots of things that make a good day a great day." I giggle after I say it. Ben has made every day a great day since we started dating. We walk hand in hand to the Brownstone next door to the shop. Ben helped me get a great deal on it after he, Paula, and I bought the building for the business. He helped me secure the loan on it and, although he owns his own place still, he spends all his free time with me.

"I was thinking," he says as I open the door, and we usher all the dogs inside.

"Uh-oh," I say and laugh. "Last time you were thinking, I bought a building."

"Come. Let's talk," he says. He leads me into the sunny alcove beside the office. I have it set up as my yoga and meditation den. Ben settles himself onto a large pillow on the floor. He sits cross-legged and beckons for me to join him. I sit, hesitant at first. The words "let's talk" have never been good in the past.

"What is it?" I say tentatively.

Ben stares deeply into my eyes. "We've had a lot of fun these past few months. We've become quite the team."

I nod, still unsure of where he's going with this.

"But," he starts. He pauses and stares at me intently.

"But?"

"But I want to be with you all the time," he says.

"I know. Is this about the hours I work? I don't see that changing," I say quietly.

"I wouldn't dream of it. You've done amazing things here. I want you to be involved and as excited as you have been these past few weeks for the rest of your life." Ben grabs my hands in his.

"Then what's the but for?" I ask. I fight the urge to pull my hands back.

"The but is about our, uh, living situation. I kind of thought since we're together all the time, maybe I should just move the rest of my

EPILOGUE – 6 MONTHS LATER

clothes in here." Ben's voice is low and hesitant. He is looking at me intently, waiting to see my reaction.

"You mean, live here?" I ask.

"Well, yes," he says. "I mean. If you want me here. I know that I want to be here. In fact, I don't want to be anywhere else. But I understand that this is a big decision."

"Yes!" I exclaim. "Yes! I want you here. Now and always."

Ben smiles in relief. I admire his teeth and dimple and smooth skin. His eyes dance in excitement, and his hands squeeze mine tightly.

"I could rent out my place. Earn some extra money for us. Maybe take a nice vacation once The Perfect Moment is running smoothly again," Ben says. He fidgets nervously.

"Yeah, sure. That would be great. I'd like that," I say.

"Marissa, I'm not very good at this. I don't know what to say. I'm awkward, and I get shy when we talk about feelings." Ben stares at me as he speaks. His eyes search mine.

"I'm not too good at it either," I admit. I wonder what he is getting all nervous about. I mean, we are just talking about moving in together, right?

"I know, and I know you've been hurt before. I want you to know. No, I need you to know that I will never, ever hurt you. All I want to do is make your life better, the same as you have been doing for me since the day we met. Even the day I got sprayed by the skunk. I can't imagine someone I'd rather awkwardly bathe in front of." Ben laughs with me.

"That was perhaps not the best day we've had," I say.

"It was a great day. It was the day I realized I want to spend the rest of my life with you." Ben grows serious.

I lean into him and run my hands through his hair.

"I want that, too," I whisper.

Ben tilts my face up and looks deeply into my eyes. "I love you with all my heart, Marissa."

"I love you too, Ben. So very much." Our lips meet and our kiss deepens. When we break away, all three dogs are staring at us from the doorway.

EPILOGUE – 6 MONTHS LATER

"It must be dinner time," Ben says, and he grins.

"Coming guys!" I laugh. "Geez. Not even five minutes of alone time, huh?"

Minnie yips in excitement, and Abe paws the floor expectantly. Mickey yawns, disinterested.

"Does our love bore you, Mickey?" asks Ben.

Mickey barks in response. Ben glances at me and grins.

"What do you say we finish this discussion over some wine in bed tonight? Our bed?" I ask.

Ben kisses me lightly and nods.

"Yeah." He says tenderly. "I'd like that."

ADOPTING DOZER WITH HEART

CHAPTER 1

"Dozer! Slow down!" I yank on Dozer's leash for the fifth time since we've stepped out of my apartment. My tug does nothing. Dozer barely acknowledges that I'm there. He sees a bird, and he runs, dragging me along behind him. I land, face-down in the muddy park, and sigh. Dozer turns and looks at me, his comical face tilted sideways in concern. He walks back to me and sniffs me, whimpering.

"Yeah, I'm okay, buddy, but you can't drag me like that. I can't wait until training school starts next week. I can't imagine what you'll be like full-grown." I sigh and get up. I have mud on my leggings, and my shirt is crumpled and full of leaves.

"'Get a Bullmastiff,' they said," I grumble under my breath. "'It'll be fun,' they said."

The truth is, it is fun when he's not dragging me around the park, that is. I got him from a rescue center a week and a half ago. I wasn't looking to adopt a dog his size but, when I saw his expressive, soulful eyes, I knew he was the one for me.

I limp over to a park bench and sit down, swiping at the mud on my leggings. So much for stopping by Café Delicioso for a quick coffee and one of their heavenly donuts.

There isn't really anywhere to leave Dozer anyway, I muse. I always sit outside when I can but, even then, I can foresee lots of issues with him being tied to the fence beside me. Dozer weighs seventy pounds already, and he is not even close to fully grown! No, my light-hearted jaunts around the city with him will have to wait until he is fully trained.

"Let's go home, bud," I say. Dozer sits and watches me get up, and I pick a few leaves from my shirt. He is calm as can be right now, until the next squirrel runs past, that is. I look around and contemplate my options. I could take the park route all the way back the way we came. There are fewer people, so there's less of a chance for Dozer to jump on someone, but there are more squirrels and a greater chance for him to drag me through the mud again. The other option is going through town. It is shorter but busier and way more stimulating for a puppy like Dozer. Still, though, there are fewer squirrels, which might mean Dozer will walk at a decent speed.

I quickly deliberate. Finally, I opt for the route through town. Dozer seems to be better-behaved when there are people around. In the park, he acts like life is a free-for-all buffet of excitement. I'm so grateful he starts obedience school next week. The rescue agency set me up with an obedience trainer. The lady there, Jenn, told me that Dozer is a handful and that he would need to be trained sooner than later. Although the class was already full, Jenn was able to pull some strings and get me in. This is a small fact that I am grateful for beyond all measure. The next round of classes starts in a month and a half, and I'm pretty sure that there's no way I'd make it that long with this crazy dog dragging me around.

Dozer is well-behaved for the first ten minutes. He walks beside me calmly, his large feet padding with the awkward stumbles of a puppy. We're right in front of the café when his calm demeanor takes a turn. Dozer's ears perk up as he sees a bird sitting on the tree beside the café patio. I hold his leash tightly and brace myself.

"Dozer, slow down," I command. He glances at me and, for a second, I think I have him under control.

My delusion quickly ends when he turns and bolts toward the tree. His big feet get tangled in his leash, and he lurches about like a broken marionette before stumbling and tripping toward the one solo table outside of the protection of the café fence.

I yank his leash, horrified as he comically falls onto the man sitting at the table.

"Dozer!" I gasp.

Dozer throws his entire weight at the table in response to his name. The flimsy café table gets knocked sideways, and the man sitting at it grapples with his chair and the table in a desperate attempt not to lose his coffee and donut. He manages to save the coffee but the donut lands right beside Dozer who gratefully gulps it down in one massive gulp.

The man stands and glares at me and then at Dozer who is lying beside the sideways table looking perfectly pleased with himself and the treat he just acquired.

"I'm so sorry," I gasp mortified. "He's a puppy. I'm so sorry. I'll get you another donut."

"Don't worry about it," the man says curtly. "Maybe next time get a dog that you can control! Or go to obedience school, for crying out loud."

"He starts next week," I say quietly, sure that my face has flushed a deep crimson. "It can't start soon enough."

The man looks at me coolly for a second. I feel like I'm under a microscope with his intense stare. His hazel eyes seem to bore holes in me, and I desperately wish the sidewalk would swallow me whole.

"I'm sorry," I whisper again, aware that everyone at the café is staring at me.

Dozer rights himself and sits obediently next to me. I feel my shoulders sag in defeat. Maybe getting a dog was a bad idea after all.

The man bends down and scratches Dozer behind the ears. His face softens, and I notice how good-looking he is. His chiseled cheekbones move into a slight grin when Dozer looks up and licks his hand.

"He's a good-looking fellow," the man says. "By the way, my name is Mark."

"Hi, Mark," I murmur. "I'm Alisha."

"Hi, Alisha. I'm sorry I was so curt. It's been one of those days, you know?"

"I sure do!" I say. I'm grateful he has given me a chance to apologize. I feel better already, even though I still probably owe this man a donut and more apologies.

"Would you like to sit? Have a donut with me?" Mark asks. His hazel eyes dig deep inside me. I feel shy all of a sudden, unsure of myself.

"Yeah, that would be nice."

Mark stands and prepares to go inside, but I catch him. "I'll get the donuts. I owe you one anyway."

The smile that spreads on Mark's face floods me with relief. His eyes crinkle in the corners in amusement and, for the first time since I left my apartment, I feel at ease. Maybe getting a dog was a good idea after all.

"Nah, I got this one. Next time, it'll be on you. What kind of donut? Coffee?" Mark laughs.

"Uhm, I want a key lime donut and a latte please," I say. "Thank you so much, by the way."

"No problem at all," Mark says, and he winks. I feel my insides burn with excitement at his small gesture of affection.

I watch his athletic body as he walks into the café. "Dozer, I need you to sit and behave. Do not screw this up for me."

Dozer looks sheepish as I tie his leash to the patio fence as close to me as possible. He settles on the ground in a sunny patch and prepares to sleep.

"Good boy," I murmur. Now if only he would stay like this the entire time I'm sitting here.

Mark comes out a second later with a tray of goodies. On it, is my latte and several donuts.

"I couldn't decide what I wanted," he admits with a laugh. "So I'm hoping you'll sample them with me."

I nod and grin. This is my idea of a great afternoon. Donuts, sunlight, and a handsome man. What's not to love?

"This is the key lime. Here we have a mud pie, and then there's the classic Boston cream. Then the donut holes. We have cherry cola, cherry Bordeaux, and cookies and cream with mocha." Mark grins like a man who's just learned how to create fire with sticks. His self-satisfied grin makes me laugh outright.

"Wow, hungry?" I giggle.

"Well. It's not every day the universe drops a fun companion by my side at the best donut place in town. When life hands you a donut sampling companion, you jump on it." Mark cuts all of the donuts into sample-size bites.

"So, what made you get a Bullmastiff?" Mark asks me as he pops a bite of warm, delicious, deep-fried goodness into his mouth.

"Well," I say slowly. How do I explain the series of events that brought me to Dozer?

"My mom died, and I really missed having a companion. My therapist suggested getting a service animal, but the waiting list was way too long, and I was off work at the time, so money was a factor but so was just sitting around waiting. So, after much deliberation, I got Dozer. He is a rescue from the local place here, and it just seemed like a good fit, even if he wasn't exactly what I was looking for. For one, I wanted a dog that was trained. But I fell in love with him, and the rescue gave me a discount on his training so here we are. He's a good boy, and I'm glad I made the choice I did. Even though his antics are embarrassing as hell." I take a bite of the key lime donut and grin.

"Wow," says Mark. "I'm so sorry about your mom. I lost my dad a few years ago. My boys, Rick and Morty, helped me get through that."

"Rick and Morty?"

"Yeah, I have two Labradoodles that I rescued a couple of years ago. I named them after my nephew's favorite cartoon. My dad was the one that got him into it."

"That's so cool."

"Yeah, they're the loves of my life." Mark smiles self-consciously as he says it.

"I get that," I say. "It feels like Dozer is mine. I mean, no relationship on the planet can take as much time or patience as he requires!"

We both laugh. Mark opens his mouth to say something and then seems to hesitate.

Is he going to ask me out? I wonder. I secretly hope he does. It's been a long time since I've gone out with anyone, much less someone that seems interesting. I was the sole caregiver for my mom when she was sick, and a lot of my friends moved on without me. My last relationship ended over a year ago and, although he was a decent enough guy, he wasn't the right fit for me. We lasted three months before calling it quits.

"These donuts are so good." I shove a small piece into my mouth and chew slowly. "There are few pleasures in life like a hand-crafted baked good."

"I could not agree more," Mark says, and he laughs. He takes a sip of his coffee and looks at me quizzically.

"Thank you, again," I say. I sound awkward. I feel awkward. Like I am trying to fill the silence.

"Stop that Alisha," I chide myself. *"Why am I so awkward with everyone?"*

"This is fun. I'm glad Dozer decided to knock me over." Mark smiles at me. Dozer raises his head at the mention of his name.

"Go to sleep, bud," I say to him. I scratch his ears, and he lies back down, contented. I can hardly believe this is the same dog that drags me around the park on our daily walks. He is such a gentle soul. Dozer really is an angel given to me at a time when I needed someone. "So why were you having one of those days? You said so after Dozer unceremoniously introduced us by falling on you."

"Just work stuff. I'm a project manager and everything that could have gone wrong this morning did. Just a series of comedic events, really. Anyway. It's fine. Donuts make everything better. And so does good company."

Mark and I talk as we sip our beverages and nibble the delectable donuts. Three hours later, I glance at my watch and gasp.

"I have to get going," I tell him. "I have someone meeting me at my condo to buy my mom's hospital bed."

"Oh, okay. Do you know the buyer? Do you want me to come and make sure it's safe?" Mark asks. "I mean, not that you know me, but I just read somewhere that it's better to have someone with you…" Mark turns red as he speaks. "Sorry, I'm assuming you don't have someone. Also, you have Dozer. I guess the last thing you need is some random guy mansplaining safety to you."

I grin at Mark's amusing fumble and his attempt to catch himself. It's nice that he cares, even if his approach is a little cringe-worthy.

"Relax! I appreciate the gesture," I say. "I have Dozer, and I have security in the building. Thank you, though. I really do appreciate the thoughtfulness."

"No matter how poorly thought out it was?" Mark grins wryly. "It was lovely to meet you. I hope we'll bump into each other again. It's been fun."

I stand and untie Dozer who immediately jumps up and puts his two front paws on Mark. The big dog leans into him, a signature Dozer move.

"Aw, he's giving you a hug," I exclaim. "He's the only dog I've ever met that seems to imitate human hugs when we leave someone."

"He's adorable," Mark says as he wraps his arms around Dozer. Dozer rests his head on Mark's shoulder and smiles.

"Well. Hopefully, I'll see you again soon," I say.

"Yeah, I'd like that," Marks says.

"Can I give you my number? Maybe we can go to the dog park. Once this goof is trained, of course." I fumble over my words as I speak.

"Oh, yeah, I'd love that. You can meet Rick and Morty," Mark says. I recite my number, and he punches it into his phone.

"I'd love to." I gather Dozer's leash in my hand.

"Great! I'll give you a call."

I walk away happy. Dozer's behavioral issues turned out to be a good thing today.

CHAPTER 2

Mark calls me the next day after work to ask me if I want to go to the park with him.

"Sure! You know Dozer, though… I won't have a lot of time to hang out chasing that goofball around. Plus, it's supposed to rain, I think. Not that I mind. Just thought I'd mention it."

"Why am I so weird and awkward with guys?" My brain chastises me as I stutter and ramble into the phone.

"Let's take our chances," Mark says. "I mean if you want to go…"

"I do! I'm sorry. I'm just awkward at this. I never know what to say. Even before all the drama in my life happened. I guess I'm just a dork at heart. One thing I am good at is laughing at myself. There was a time in my life when I considered trying to be a stand-up comedian but, in the end, it didn't work out. Life has a funny way of happening in spite of yourself."

"So, let's take our chances on some pesky rain. Do you want to meet at the boardwalk, and we can walk to the park? Maybe do the section by the water? Or in the park? Whichever."

"Yeah, that sounds amazing!" I agree.

I let Mark go and race around my condo like a maniac. How is it possible that Mark and I both are so shy and amateurs at this dating thing? Is this even a date? I have no idea, but the one thing I did learn from losing my mom is to enjoy life as much as possible and to go with the flow. And I intend to do just that.

"Dozer! I need to find something to wear!" I lament to my dog. He raises one eyebrow and regards me with interest. "Quick! Grey or maroon leggings?"

I scurry out the door half an hour later in my grey leggings and a workout shirt, rain jacket, and runners with my hair and makeup neatly done. I get to the boardwalk with moments to spare. Mark is sitting on a bench with two large Labradoodles resting calmly by his feet. Dozer barks and yanks at his leash.

"Dozer, stop. Please. Sit!" Dozer sits for a second before tugging at his lead again.

"I see Dozer is ready for this!" Mark says. He stands and stretches. Two dogs I assume are Ricky and Morty both sit up and wait patiently.

"Yeah, like everything," I say as I laugh.

"So, I was thinking, how do you feel about doing the walk around the sea wall instead of through the park? It looks like the rain is going to hold off until later. According to the news station, it's just going to be light rain, anyway. We just might have to be careful. The sea-walk does get slippery sometimes."

I hesitate and glance at the one grey cloud in the sky.

"Just do it," I think to myself. *"Stop being so scared of everything. You've been like this since Mom died. Take a chance!"*

"Yeah, sure. Let's do it."

Mark grins, and we begin walking. Dozer pulls lightly at his lead, but he seems to want to be with the pack of us, so he walks closer to me than normal.

"I think he's imitating your two," I say in amazement. "Do Bullmastiffs do that?"

Mark watches him with amusement. "I'm not sure, but it does seem like that's what he's doing."

We get partway around the sea wall walk, and then the rain starts. At first, it's a light downfall. We laugh and keep walking. Before long, it becomes a torrential downpour. The path along the water is drenched and slippery. The waves crash into the retaining wall with a fury I've never seen.

"Wow, I think we should try and find somewhere to stay until this slows down!" Mark says over the roar of the howling wind. "It got dark fast!"

I nod in agreement and look around. There's nowhere to go that is out of the wind and rain. On one side of us is a steep cliff face, unclimbable and unpassable, and on the other is the water.

"How about this little overhang?" Marks says. He points to an indent in the rock wall. It has a deep overhang and an area big enough for us to all fit, albeit tightly.

I nod, and we walk cautiously toward the small shelter.

"Wow, that is not what I would call a 'light shower,'" laughs Mark. "More like a tropical storm in the non-tropics!"

I nod and shuffle my feet to make room for Dozer to lay down. I am pressed against the back of the small cavern, and all three dogs sit at our feet. Mark is pressed right up against me in the tight space.

"This is nuts," I say, and I watch warily as the rain begins to look as though it is falling sideways from the heavy winds.

"No kidding. Weather guy sure was off today!" I laugh and look up at Mark. He looks handsome in the gloomy shadows, his cheekbones prominent and sculpted. The muscles in his arms press against his long-sleeve athletic shirt, and his abs are tight, flat, and well-formed. Mark glances down at me and grins. His eyes turn serious as he looks at me. My hair drips down my face and onto my shirt. I should have worn a hat, I muse. Too bad Dozer didn't tell me that when I asked for his advice about my outfit. I smile to myself.

"You have a beautiful smile," Mark says quietly.

My face gets hot. "Thank you."

"What are you smiling at?"

"Well, I asked Dozer earlier for advice on what to wear today, and he failed to mention a hat. I think, considering the amount of water pouring out of my hair, that maybe a hat would have been a good idea," I say. I shake my head slightly and rain droplets fly from my long, brown hair.

"Bad Dozer," Mark says huskily. I smile slowly as he gently pushes my wet hair off my face.

Dozer glances up at us, his face questioning. When he sees we're busy, he lowers his head to his paws again.

Mark's fingers linger on my cheek as he moves my hair. His eyes crinkle at the edges as our eyes lock. I find myself looking deeply into his eyes, unable to look away. The gold flecks in his hazel eyes seem to dance with the inclement weather and moving shadows. Before I have time to think about my actions, I stand on my tippy-toes, my face close to his. Mark takes the cue and leans into me. His soft lips meet mine and press against me. I exhale sharply and deepen the kiss. You only live once, after all.

When the kiss breaks, Mark looks at me intently.

"That was amazing."

"Yeah, it was." I agree. I drop my eyes in embarrassment because of my flushed face.

"I'm glad Dozer decided to jump on me." Mark says Dozer's name a bit too loudly. Dozer stands and, before I can stop him, he bounds out of the makeshift cave onto the slippery path. All four of his feet slide out from under him, and he skids dangerously close to the water's edge.

"Dozer!" I shout, alarmed. "Come!"

Dozer looks confused as rain pelts down on him and, before I know what is happening, he is sliding off the side of the path toward the water.

Mark leaps into action. He dives at the dog, lands in front of him, and grabs his collar. Rick and Morty watch with interest as their person pulls the big dog back onto the path and to safety.

"Oh, my gosh! Mark! Are you okay? Dozer!"

Mark hobbles back to the overhang wincing. Dozer lays down as if nothing just happened.

"I think I fell on my arm wrong," Mark says. He holds his wrist and winces.

"Oh, gosh. I'll drive you to get x-rays," I say. Mark nods looking defeated and somewhat unhappy.

We stand in silence as the rain eventually slows and then stops. We all walk slowly back to the boardwalk and then to our respective cars.

"Do you want me to take you to get it looked at?" I ask.

Mark shakes his head. "No, I think I've had enough of today," he says. He smiles ruefully. "Seems like every time I see you, your dog hurts me."

"It's not his fault!" I exclaim.

"No, it's never the dog's fault. It was a stupid idea bringing an untrained dog here, though. That's on me." Mark holds his wrist and winces. The pain in his face is palpable.

"Thank you for saving him, and I am so sorry. Again," I say. The tears sting my eyes and threaten to fall.

Mark's face softens, and he looks at me with sad eyes. "Look, it's not anyone's fault, but I have to go get this looked at. I'm pretty sure it's broken." Mark opens the back door with his left hand and Rick and Morty climb in. "I'm sorry I snapped at you. Totally uncalled for."

"Please, let me know how it is. If you won't let me drive you," I say as Mark gets into the driver's side. "I am so sorry."

I watch in dismay as he drives away. Dozer whimpers as he watches his friends in the backseat.

I sigh. "Thanks, Dozer," I grumble. He looks at me with sad eyes. "I know, bud. It's not your fault. Tuesday cannot come soon enough for that darned obedience school."

CHAPTER 3

Mark doesn't call me until the next day. I leave three messages for him before he calls me back.

"Hey."

"Hi! Are you okay?"

"Yeah, I am. Broken arm. Clean break though, thank goodness. Makes working hard, though."

"Mark…"

"Don't. It's fine. I know it's no one's fault. I just have to figure out how the heck I'm going to get through the next six weeks in a cast, now."

"Is there anything I can do to help?" I fidget as I ask. I hope he says yes. I really feel terrible about what happened.

"Maybe. My assistant is away for the next three days so I might just take you up on that. What's your schedule like this week?"

I mentally take note of my calendar. It's a pretty open week. I'm still on part-time hours at work and, other than Dozer's obedience training, I don't have any appointments.

"Pretty good, actually. I work remotely and only part-time right now. Other than Dozer's obedience training…"

"Which you must attend," Mark says as he laughs.

"Yes. You better believe it. So, can I help. It's my fault you're injured anyway. What do you need to be done? I have a large office where you could work if you wanted. Or… you tell me. Sorry. I just really want to make this better."

"I can't type. That's the main thing," Mark says it thoughtfully. I can almost hear the wheels turning in his brain as he tries to make sense of his current predicament.

"Why don't you come over for lunch, and you can check out the office? Show me what you need. I made a lasagna last night. We can have that."

Mark agrees and, an hour later, he's buzzing up from the security desk.

"Wow, this place is gorgeous."

"Thanks! I bought it my second year out of university. I got it at pre-build prices. It's a two-bedroom plus den they call it but look at the den! It's a full bedroom basically." I beam with pride as I show Mark around my place.

"Wow, what do you do again?" Mark looks at me with interest. His hazel eyes twinkle.

"I'm the director of marketing at Intel-I-Gent. Or I was anyway. I'm still on leave since looking after my mom."

"The big software company?"

"Yeah, the one and only."

Mark whistles, impressed. Most people are impressed with my title. Most are also a little shocked since I kind of come off as the slightly-goofy girl next door.

"Wow! Impressive. Well, the boring assistant stuff I have lined up for you will be a breeze then! If the monotony doesn't kill you."

I laugh, and Mark joins in. "I like monotony, nowadays."

"I bet."

Dozer ambles over and sniffs Mark. He nudges against his cast and looks up at him with woeful eyes.

"Yeah, bud. This is all you," Mark says. He scratches Dozer's ear playfully. Dozer barks and lowers himself as though he's looking to play. For a second, I think he is going to jump on Mark, and I gasp.

ADOPTING DOZER WITH HEART

"Dozer! No! Sit." Dozer sits and looks at me as if to say, *I'm a good boy*.

"Good boy!" I praise. I hand him a small treat from my pocket.

"Wow," says Mark. "Maybe you can teach a dog new tricks."

"You can when the reward is freeze-dried meat!" I say and laugh. "Seriously, though. This training class cannot come soon enough."

Mark absently brushes the top of Dozer's head with the tips of his fingers.

"Ready for lunch?" I ask brightly. I haven't had anyone over since long before my mom got sick. I'm nervous, but how much worse can this get? I mean, I've already knocked this guy over, and he broke his arm rescuing my wayward animal. What have I got to lose at this point?

I serve the lasagna with a salad and garlic bread.

"This is great!" Mark says as he takes a bite.

"I'm glad. I can cook better than I can train dogs," I say ruefully. "Mark, I am so sorry…"

"Stop. It's okay. I appreciate the help you're giving me, anyway."

Mark puts his fork down and looks at me. His eyes seem to penetrate right into my soul, and I wonder for a second if I am going to burst into flames of desire. I think back to the kiss in the cave and shiver slightly, and then I remember Dozer and the way the kiss ended. I am lucky this man is talking to me, much less that he's still so agreeable after everything that went on. I drop my eyes and continue eating.

"Do you want to work here, or are you supposed to be onsite? What exactly do you need?" I ask Mark after the dishes are cleared. We're sitting in front of his laptop at my spacious desk. "I should be able to access your files, emails, and schedules from my computer with remote access."

"Basically, I can't type. I can still visit the site, and I can still do it in person although I usually have someone to take notes as well, but no matter. We can work from my office too. It's basically within walking distance from here. We just need to get you access to all my stuff, and then we can play it by ear."

"I can do that," I say quickly.

"Okay. Well, thank you. Let's get it set up then. My assistant should be back in a few days. She's gone to visit her mom right now."

I nod and bite my lip. The knowledge that I will never be able to do that again hits me suddenly. I drop my eyes and feel the sting as I fight for composure.

"I'm sorry. I know how hard it is," Mark says. He looks at me with empathy, and I smile in spite of myself. He really is a gem of a man to look at.

"It's okay," I mumble. "Let's get this sorted out so you can get back to work."

Less than an hour later, I'm set up on his network and ready to be his assistant.

"What's first, boss?" I joke.

"First, I need to respond to a bunch of emails for clients and contractors. Then I have to update our investors on some things, and that'll be it for today."

I type as Mark leans over my shoulder dictating. I find his good looks hovering over me a bit distracting, but I force myself to focus. I'm sure that the fiasco by the water ended any chance of Mark and I ever kissing again much less dating.

We finish in record time. Mark looks satisfied as I hit send on the last email.

"Well, all done," I say cheerfully. "I should wrap this up early. I have to take this guy out for a walk, and then I think it's time for a bath and bed for me."

"You are a wild party," says Mark as he winks.

"I know. I know. I always go to bed early. Just doesn't seem like there's much going on past nine p.m. most nights. Plus, Dozer likes to get up at five a.m." I scratch his ears as I speak. "I'll see you tomorrow?"

"Yeah, sure. I have a meeting at ten. If you're able, can you take notes, and then I'll treat you to lunch?"

"What about Dozer, though? I don't have daycare for him booked."

"I have a caregiver for my two. He can stay with her. Julia's great.

She works with the Training Academy. Is that where he'll be doing his training?"

"Yeah! I've heard they're great!"

"They sure are. Well, then it's settled. I'll see you tomorrow at nine a.m. here?" Mark folds his hands in mock smugness over his chest. His face is stern for a second before he breaks into a grin. "Not very intimidating am I, with this massive cast?"

"No, you're not. But I'll see you then." Mark gives me a quick hug of thanks and leaves. I bounce out the door with Dozer and head to the park. On the way, I call my best friend Amy.

"Hey, girl, what's up?" Amy asks on the second ring.

"Nothing. Met a cute guy. Dozer stole his donut. He took me on a date. I broke his arm. The end. How about you?"

"Wait, what?" Amy laughs. "I'm going to need some more details on this one."

I tell Amy the story, and she laughs hysterically. "So, let me get this straight. There is a man. A project manager, no less, wandering around the city right now with a broken arm because he went on a date with you?"

"Yeah, and, to make matters worse, his assistant is away, and he can't type. Or do anything else that requires the use of his right hand," I lament. "So, I agreed to be his assistant for a few days. Good thing I'm off work. All this socializing is turning into a full-time job."

Amy laughs loudly into the phone. I wince and pull my ear away. "Geeze, girl, that's my ear."

This makes Amy laugh even harder. Her giggles turn into guffaws and pretty soon we're both chortling like hyenas.

"Director of marketing to an assistant for l-o-o-o-o-o-v-v-v-e!" shrieks Amy. "What could possibly go wrong?"

"You mean that hasn't already? I don't know. I guess I could somehow concuss him or blow up his car." I snigger.

"Blow up his car," gasps Amy as her laughter turns to hysterical wheeziness. "Yeah, that's date two!"

"Maybe three. Can't give away all my secrets before then!" This sets us off into another gale of laughter.

"Seriously, though," says Amy. "You really think it's done with him just because of the whole arm thing?"

"I don't know if it was ever a thing but, yeah, I'd say so. Why?"

"Because I have a guy I want to set you up with, if you're available, still."

"I might be. I don't know. I'm not sure I'm equipped to date. Let me make it through this week without any other calamity before I decide, okay?"

Amy messages me the next day asking me if she can give her friend my number. I shake my head before answering.

"What's that?" asks Mark. "You look like you just swallowed something sour."

"Oh, nothing. My friend, Amy. She wants to set me up with someone. I keep telling her no," I say quickly. Mark is silent for a second. I glance up at him, and he is staring at me intently. His eyes are darker than normal, and I wonder if I've said something wrong. I mean, we're not dating, right? A kiss and then breaking the man's arm doesn't count as a commitment, does it?

"So, what's next?" I ask him. The morning meeting has ended, and I've taken the notes and written and sent two emails as follow-ups. Mark looks pained every time he asks me to do something.

"I hate being so useless," he complains after the third and final email goes out. "At least, let me pay you for your time. Or something."

"Pay me?" I ask incredulously.

"I mean. No, that's the wrong answer, isn't it? I don't mean it in a bad way. Is it bad? I just mean this is all so weird. I hate that I can't use my arm at all. The doctor said it won't be until the third week that I can do the things I'm used to doing. Everything is a struggle. I'm sorry. I must sound like a whiny jerk to you."

"A little," I admit. "But I get it. I'd be the same if the shoe was on the other foot. And anyway, it's mostly my fault you're even in this predicament."

"Not really. It was an accident," says Mark. "What do you feel like for lunch?"

"I don't know," I answer honestly. We're in a part of town I don't know very well.

"How about Mexican? There's an authentic taco place down the street if you want."

"Yeah, that's awesome," I say. "I haven't had a real taco since I backpacked through Mexico a few years ago."

"Wow," Mark says. "You've done a lot!"

"I guess. I want to travel more. But I'm planning to stick to road trips for the moment since Dozer is my main focus right now."

We stroll to the taco place. Mark orders us each three of his favorites and some guacamole and homemade chips. The restaurant is a small hole-in-the-wall type, the kind that you might pass by if you didn't know it was there. Inside, the tiles are cracked but clean. An older Mexican lady stands in the kitchen churning out tacos and guacamole just like her mom did back in Mexico City.

"These are so authentic!" I exclaim as I shovel one in my face. Mark struggles to get it up to his mouth with one hand. He finally succeeds and grins in victory.

"Victory shall yet be mine!" he says as he laughs.

"Do you need help?" I ask.

"Oh, gosh. No chance. I'm not willing to get to that level of need." Mark's left hand wobbles as he carefully delivers the taco to his mouth. He gets most of it in his mouth. A bit of sauce misses and dribbles down his handsome chin.

"So close," I say and pass him a napkin.

"And yet so far."

We both laugh. He chews thoughtfully as I shovel chips and guacamole in my mouth. "What's the plan for this afternoon?"

"Isn't Dozer's training tonight?" asks Mark.

"Yeah, but I can help you until three if you want."

"It's okay. I don't have much going on today," Mark says.

"Oh. Okay," I say. My shoulders deflate slightly. I was looking forward to spending more time with Mark.

"I'm glad we got to have lunch, though. Despite it being like you're eating with a three-year-old." Mark grins ruefully as another taco falls apart on its way to his mouth.

After lunch, I head home to get Dozer. I don't want to be late for our first night. The class goes surprisingly well, and I'm left with confidence that he can be an obedient dog, after all.

Mark calls me the next morning to tell me that his assistant is coming back a day early since he needs her but that he could use my help for part of the day. I feel a pang of sadness when I realize this might be my last day with him.

"I don't get why he won't ask me out," I grumble to Amy on my way to his office. "We seemed to have so much chemistry."

"Maybe he doesn't know you're interested. Have you done anything to make him think you might not be?"

"No… I don't think so. I can't think of anything," I say. "I don't know. I'm not very good at this, apparently."

"Don't say that. Maybe just stay in contact with him and see? Perhaps he's shy. Especially after you tried to kill him…"

I laugh. "I did not try to kill him, for crying out loud. But yeah, I can see where that would be intimidating."

"Whatever. Tomato, Tomaaaato."

"Anyway, gotta go. I'm here."

I walk into the office. In my head, I rehearse what I'll say when I leave tonight. Will I pledge to be his friend? That seems like the best approach until I know how he feels.

"Hey, Mark!" I say brightly. Mark smiles when he sees me. I love the way his eyes crinkle in happiness. It brings me joy. My heart flip flops when I look at him. That has to be a sign of something, right?

"Hey! So today I was thinking I'd just get you to wrap up the emails so that Amelia can jump right in when she's back tomorrow. She's worked for me a long time now, so she'll know what needs to be done. Does that work? I know it's boring stuff, but I really do appreciate the help. My hand is still so swollen from the break!" Mark lifts his arm for me to see. The cast seems more spacious than it was, but Marks' fingers still look like little sausages poking out of it. Little, chubby, red, painful sausages. I cringe again and curse myself for the whole series of events from that day.

"Mark… I'm so sorry," I say again.

"Don't be! I'm fine with it. Call it an adventure. Every day is a new challenge with the left. Like how do I button my pants or answer my phone? I am shockingly un-ambidextrous."

Mark laughs easily, and I grin along with him. We work side by side throughout the day. I mentally prepare what I'm going to say when I leave for the eight-hundredth time as we ponder details for an upcoming project he has going on.

After work, we sit and chat on the plush couches Mark has in his waiting area.

"So how was training school?" Mark asks.

"It was great! You should see how well Dozer did. He's going to be a superstar!"

"He already is," says Mark.

We sit in silence for what feels like an eternity. I can hear my heart thumping in my ears, and the butterflies dance in my stomach. Mark sips his coffee as both of us start and then stop speaking.

"So, uh, I've had a lot of fun working with you, even if the conditions, to begin with, were less than amazing," I say.

"Me, too. We should definitely hang out again," Mark says.

"Yeah. Hang out. For sure. Like friends," I agree.

"Yeah, like that," Mark says. He looks at me intently and then smiles brightly. His eyes crinkle at the edges, and I feel my insides swoon for a brief second.

I leave feeling defeated and confused. Does he just want to be friends? I'm not sure but it seemed like he agreed with me.

CHAPTER 4

The next few days fly by quickly. I'm working part-time again and spending the rest of my time working with Dozer. I really want to get his training right. Dozer is a lovable dog, and I want the rest of the world to see that, not the misbehaving giant that he currently is.

Dozer has a special graduation from the school several weeks later. He is graduating at the top of his class, he's obedient, and he's well-focused. I am excited about his graduation, and I text Mark to let him know.

My phone rings a second after I hit send. Mark's face shows up on the caller ID.

"Hello?"

"Hey! It's Mark! I haven't heard from you in a bit. It's nice to hear your voice. That's super-exciting about Dozer! Maybe now you'll be able to adopt more fur babies."

"Uh, maybe. I'm not in the market at the moment. How are things with you? Arm better?"

"Not fully but getting there. Everything is great. I've missed hearing your voice."

"Well, we have texted a few times. What's new?"

"Not much. New work project. How about you?"

"Dozer's graduating, and I'm back at work three-quarters of the time."

"That's great!"

"Yeah…" I hesitate. How I long to tell him that I miss seeing him or that I have a massive crush on him. I want him to know this, to read my mind. I'm just not sure I can handle the rejection if I say it and he feels differently.

"Can I come to Dozer's graduation?" Mark asks me. I force myself back to the present time.

"Yeah, I'd like that a lot."

Mark arrives as promised for Dozer's graduation. He claps and cheers when Dozer and I get his diploma. Afterward, we stand by my car awkwardly making small-talk.

"Well," I say. "I should go, I guess. We should definitely have coffee and donuts soon, though."

"Yes. We should. Alisha…" Mark starts and then pauses.

"Yes?"

He seems to hesitate. I wonder vaguely what he's thinking but I'm scared to ask. Mark looks so handsome standing in the sun. His dark hair is cropped close to his head, the ends curling delicately. I imagine running my hands through it again like I did the night he kissed me. His eyes sparkle, and his straight white smile makes me smile back at him. I long to touch his soft lips again, one more time.

"Nothing. It was really great to see you," he finishes lamely.

"You too," I say. "I have to get going. I'm meeting Amy for drinks at La Fontaine later. We'll be at the bar if you want to stop by."

Mark hesitates. "I might. But I kind of have plans. Let me see if I can cancel."

"Oh, yeah, of course. Well, whenever. Another time," I say abruptly. My mind pictures Mark on a date with someone and, for a second, I see red.

"He's not even yours to consider," my mind reminds me. *"It was one kiss. One beautiful and intense, passion-filled kiss."*

"I'll see what I can do. Work's been nuts."

"I understand. Another time."

I leave and drive home quickly. Dozer and I take a long nap, and I wake up sad but ready to meet up with Amy.

"Okay, Dozer. First day home alone. No crate. You got this? I want my condo to look just like it does now. Clean and nothing broken. Albeit it's a bit messy. Maybe you can clean up for me?" I laugh and Dozer cocks his head at me. I glance around the condo and mentally make a note to put my blankets and books away. I've always been neat. The few items out of place are out of the ordinary for me, although I doubt anyone else would think anything of them. I kiss Dozer's nose and head out the door.

"Hey, girl! What's new?" Amy asks as she hugs me.

"Not much. Dozer graduated. I'm back at work mostly. Oh, and I saw Mark earlier."

"Mark? Hot guy you almost killed?"

"Yeah. Him."

"Wow, and how was that?"

"Weird. He's so good-looking, and I really like him. But I'm guessing he doesn't feel the same. I invited him to meet us tonight, but he said he has plans."

"What kind of plans? Like another girl or like 'I work all day every day?'"

I shrug and take a swig of my beer. "I don't know. He didn't say. I didn't ask."

"Forget that guy then, I guess."

I nod, and Amy and I clink our beers together. We chat as the restaurant gets more crowded as the evening descends. Amy and I get wedged closely together at the bar as other patrons hurry to their tables or crowd around the bar waiting for their tables.

"It got busy in here," I say. I munch on a seafood tower with Amy. It's nice to treat myself to something decadent.

"Don't look now," she says suddenly.

"At?" I crane my neck around to see what she is looking at. She yanks my arm, and I jerk my head back.

"I said *don't look*. A hot guy is staring at you from the end of the bar." Amy looks over my shoulder and pauses. "He's coming this way."

A second later, I feel a tap on my shoulder. Amy eyeballs the person doing the tapping.

"Mind if I join you?" a familiar voice says. I pause for a second. Is that...?

I turn around and find myself face to face with Mark. He is dressed in well-fitted jeans and a sweater that showcases his fit physique.

"Mark!" I exclaim. Amy's eyes widen at the mention of his name.

"Hi..."

"Hey, I thought you had plans?"

"I did. Work dinner. I bailed and said I was sick."

"So, it wasn't a date?"

"What? No, of course not."

"Oh." I feel foolish. "I mean, you never said it was a date. I just assumed, I guess."

"I haven't dated anyone in a long time. Why did you think that? Did I say something that made you think that?" Mark stutters slightly, and I laugh again at how awkward he and I both are.

Amy is watching our exchange with amusement. Finally, she stands and gestures to her stool.

"I'm going to hit the lady's room. Mark, have a seat. It seems like you two have a lot to talk about."

Mark stands in front of her stool, his hands clasped together.

"It's nice to see you," I say. "Thanks for coming."

"The reason I came..." Mark pauses and seems to think. I wonder if he is going to finish his sentence. The intense way he is looking at me is sending signals of lust to my nether regions, and the butterflies in my stomach are fluttering so hard that I'm sure he can hear them. My heart thumps in my ears and in my chest.

"Is it because I invited you?"

"Yes," Mark says. "No. I came because I wanted to do this."

Mark leans into me. His large hand tenderly holds the back of my head, and his lips move toward mine. I inhale slowly, smelling his cologne and his shampoo. His lips touch mine, soft and masculine. His arm comes around me, pulling me to the edge of my stool. I kiss him passionately, with fervor. My heart hammers in excitement, and my mind buzzes as if filled with electricity. The kiss deepens, and the bar seems to disappear around us.

Finally, we break free. Mark gently runs his fingers down my cheek. He is close to me, so close that I can feel his heart hammering in his chest. Or is that my heart? I can't tell because I'm so nervous.

"I've wanted to do that since the day at the shore," Mark says.

I open my mouth, but nothing comes out. Instead, I lean into Mark's muscular body and hold him, hoping my actions are enough to show that I feel the same way.

"I didn't, though, because I thought you had no interest," he continues.

"Why would you think that?" I ask.

"You mentioned that Amy was trying to set you up with someone, and I thought that was your way of telling me that you weren't interested. In me."

"What? No. That was my way of telling you that I was interested in you. Not in someone else."

"Well," interjects Amy who has been standing beside us watching. "That's awkward."

Mark and I both laugh.

"No kidding," he says. "I would have kissed you a long time ago if I'd known. Then you said we could be friends, so I assumed that's what it was."

"No, you said it first," I argue playfully.

"Did not. I'm quite clear on what I want," Mark says firmly.

"Are you?" I tease.

"Oh, yes."

"What's that?"

"You, of course!" Mark leans in and brushes his lips softly on mine. I grin and throw my arms around him.

"Great. Because that's what I want too," I say.

"Gosh, guys. Get a room! I want to finish my beer and seafood this century!" says Amy as she laughs.

Mark grins and moves closer to me so Amy can squeeze next to us. She covers the tab, and Mark and I stroll out hand in hand with Amy in tow.

"I'm going to get a Lyft® from here guys. I'm so glad it's worked out for you. Although now I'm going to hear your name three times as much as I already do." Amy giggles. "Alisha. Love you, girl. Chat soon!" She strolls toward the Lyft® pickup spot, waving behind her as she goes.

"She's a great person," I say. "I'm lucky to have her as a friend."

"She seems great. And I'm glad you have great people. I hope she feels that I'm great for you as well."

"She's happy when I'm happy."

"And are you?"

"Yes," I say firmly. Mark puts his arms around me and pulls me close to him.

"Me too," he says. "I only wish I had known weeks ago that you feel the same as I do."

"Same," I murmur into his chest.

"But late is better than never," he finishes.

"It sure is," I agree.

We turn and walk toward my condo, hand in hand.

EPILOGUE – SIX MONTHS LATER

"Alisha?" I can hear Mark call me from the office. I bounce off the bed, startling Dozer and our new adoptee Charlotte, the dachshund.

"Yeah, babe!" I exclaim. "Where are you?"

"Garage!"

I walk swiftly to our new two-car garage and pause. Mark is standing inside it with a small bulldog puppy in his arms looking sheepish.

"Who's this?" I ask cautiously. Mark and I have agreed that we have enough dogs. Four is our limit, I had said, and he had agreed. Or so I thought.

"This is Dolly. She's a rescue. I agreed to foster her until we find her a forever home."

I take this information in slowly. Another dog. Five is a lot for any household, even one the size of ours. A lot has changed since that night by the bar. Mark and I have both rented out our condos and bought a farmhouse together. It sits on ten acres of land and has more than enough room for us and the four dogs. We keep a few chickens in the back for eggs, and I have taken to growing as many of our vegetables as I can. I also keep several beehives that produce honey, which I

EPILOGUE – SIX MONTHS LATER

sell. My mom always said she wished she could have bees, so I've named the company after her. Mom's Honey.

I'm working even fewer hours at work, the income from my condo and honey is more than enough for me to live on. I also have the investments from my mom's estate just in case I need them.

"I think Amy still wants to adopt," I say helpfully, knowing full well that Dolly is not going anywhere.

"Oh," says Mark. "Well. In that case. Yeah. Maybe? I mean, is she even home enough for a dog? Her job is full-time."

"So are most people's," I say. "And she works from home. My home."

Amy rented my condo when I moved in with Mark. She loves living centrally, and I gave her a good deal as long as she promised to stay for at least two years. It is a deal that has worked out for all of us.

"Well, that just won't work," Mark says and grins.

"Uhm, okay. Why?" I ask.

"Because. Uh. This face. Look at this face. How could you leave this face for eight hours a day?"

"Amy works at home. She wouldn't be."

"Okay. Well. I can't leave this face either. Can we consider her? Please? Rick and Morty are older and spend half their time with each other in the yard. You have Dozer and Charlotte. Oh, wait for a second. Charlotte was also a rescue you brought home. And Rick and Morty are four. That's not old at all."

"True. But let's not be hasty in the judgment," laughs Mark. He stands in front of his SUV stroking Dolly and waiting for me to do what he knows I'm going to do. Approve.

"Fine. That has to be it though Mark. I'm going to spend three-quarters of my day picking up dog poo and feeding these eating machines at the rate we're going. No more. Okay?"

"I promise. Even I know this one is pushing it."

"It sure is," I agree. "She is adorable though."

Mark brings Dolly indoors. He carefully prepares a bed for her, and he washes and fills a water bowl. She trembles slightly when he puts her down, the sights and sounds overwhelming to her. He sits next to her on the ground and strokes her gently. She sniffs the food

EPILOGUE – SIX MONTHS LATER

area, and Mark leans close to her to show her which bowl is hers. The little dog eats a few mouthfuls, chewing loudly before laying down on the rug and falling asleep. Mark pets her and lies next to her on the rug. I watch them both with amusement and affection.

"This is what a happy house should be," I muse. I fill the older dogs' bowls and, before I can put them down, Rick, Morty, and Dozer are all standing in front of me, wide-eyed and eager for their mid-afternoon meal. Charlotte follows close behind, eager to get her fair share of the bounty.

None of them even glances at Mark and Dolly until their bowls are licked clean. Only then do they become curious and sniff the little bulldog. She glances at them warily and, before she has a chance to react, Dozer licks her hard across her face. Mark laughs as Bullmastiff spit slathers the smaller dog's face.

"Nice, Dozer. Not sure she needed that kind of a bath." He laughs. I giggle at the whole situation.

"Are we going to need a bigger bed soon?" I ask, teasing him. He told me that if he ever got another dog, we would have to put two king-size beds together to accommodate us all. I look around at all of the furry bodies sitting near me. It seems like it's time for that now.

"Yes, I can do that. I've got time off after this project. I'll work on making another frame then, okay?"

I laugh and nod. "Yeah. You know how much I love my sleep, right?"

"Sure do. Don't know how, with all of the dog-snoring going on."

"Easy. Pillow over the head. It's your snoring I have the issue with!"

"I don't snore! You even said I don't!"

I shrug and walk into the kitchen laughing.

Later that evening, Mark and I sit and enjoy an evening glass of wine in our gazebo. The night is clear and crisp, and the stars are visible early on.

"It's so pretty out here," I say for what must have been the seven-hundredth time since we moved in.

"Yeah, it is. But not as pretty as you are." Mark says. His voice is quiet, husky. I can feel him staring at me intently. I glance at his handsome face and deep eyes. They're deeper than normal tonight,

EPILOGUE – SIX MONTHS LATER

and I wonder if something is wrong. He seems different, unsure of himself.

"What's..." I start but he stops me with a kiss. His lips brush mine as he drops to one knee in front of me.

"Alisha, I almost let you go because I was too shy to ask you how you felt. I'm not ever taking that chance again."

Mark's big hands fumble around under the chair he was sitting on. He finds a small box and opens it. Inside is a diamond ring. I gasp, my brain flooding with the reality of what is about to happen.

"Alisha, will you marry me?" Mark asks. His hazel eyes meet mine, shy, pleading. He looks so vulnerable kneeling in front of me that I want to wrap my arms around him and never let go.

"Yes!" I say hastily. Relief floods his handsome face, and he confidently puts the ring on my finger. It fits perfectly.

"You make me so happy," he says to me and wraps his strong arms around me tightly. I lean into him, feeling myself land in a place I never imagined possible a few months ago.

"You make me happy too," I say, and I mean it. I feel the tension melt from me in his embrace. "We may have had an awkward beginning, but you were so worth the wait."

"*We* were so worth the wait," Mark reiterates. I grin and nod.

"Yes, *we* were so worth the wait," I agree. My lips meet his, and I begin contemplating the next part of our lives together.

RESCUING ROXY WITH HEART

CHAPTER 1

Michael walked into his house to find nothing more than the painful emptiness that he had come to hate ever since his wife died. Emptiness filled the house to nearly overflowing with pain and grief. It was everywhere. It adorned the walls that no longer held framed photos because Mia had been in all of them. Seeing her beautiful face, full of life as it once had been, was too painful for him to bear. The emptiness lingered on the furniture as her favorite chair now gathered dust.

Any moment, he felt as if the dust would form into a big ball that would then form her body. Even though he knew the idea was ludicrous, he still looked for her in the empty chair. He could see her so clearly. The emptiness, absurdly, he could feel in the air. This was the same air that used to be alive with the scent of her perfume and the aroma of her cooking, but now the air was another empty space without life or fragrance. It was just... there.

Michael called out to his son, Jack, but he received no reply aside from a heavy silence devoid of words. It was devoid of everything, really.

His son wasn't home, unfortunately, but he wasn't *gone* like his wife was. Of that, Michael was sure. Or, more accurately, he hoped and believed. After the loss of his wife, he was no longer confident about life or the well-being of his loved ones, which he now considered with a pinch of skepticism. Once Mia had abandoned him on this sad earth, he'd realized that anything could happen, even the most painful and most unimaginable things.

Jack was probably off with his friends either studying or having fun. Or he might have just been trying to escape the grief that had shrouded him like a wet blanket since the loss of his mom.

Michael considered calling him to ask where he was but decided against it. The boy was old enough, and he didn't need to be micromanaged like a toddler. Michael wasn't so old that he couldn't remember how it felt to be a senior in high school. He wasn't so old that he couldn't remember how much he'd wanted to be free, to be independent, and to be his own man when he was Jack's age.

He trusted his son, and he didn't want to be the insecure father looming over him like a dark shadow. Mia's absence did that well enough. The boy was old enough to have a reasonable level of freedom, as was his right, especially given the fact that he knew that Jack was struggling just as much as Michael, himself, had been.

It had been a year since Mia died, but the pain was still heavy in their hearts. He was proud of how Jack had handled it so far and, if the boy wanted to hang out with his friends without calling to get permission, well, he had earned that right.

Michael was also careful to make sure that his paranoia and grief didn't affect his parental duties. The fact that he always felt lonely without Mia was no excuse to rob his son of the best years of his teenage life.

However, while Michael was indeed lonely, he was never alone. And as if sensing that he was missing his son, Roxy came running toward him, wagging her tail with the excitement and energy of a shooting star. Michael ran his hand across the light brown fur of the Labrador Retriever, playing with her ears before bending down to stroke her back lightly. She licked his face, and he smiled as her wet tongue lapped at his nose. He let his fingers ruffle her fur some more.

He got to his feet and walked to the basement with Roxy in tow, bouncing with joy and excitement as she followed. Roxy was the only reason why his home didn't feel empty. She was the only reason why he didn't feel absolutely alone.

Down in the basement, Michael switched on the light to reveal his man-cave. He had converted the dark, dank basement into a place of solitude with bright lights, a state-of-the-art gaming system, a small gym, a beer fridge, and a brown leather couch. When Mia was alive, she always complained that he spent too much time in his cave rather than with her. He used to think she was just being ridiculous.

They, after all, spent a lot of time together, and they were going to be together forever. They'd assumed that they had all the time in the world. However, now that she was gone, he realized that she was right. He should have stolen every opportunity he had to enjoy her presence. He'd always cherished his time with her, but, if he'd known that she would leave him so soon, he would have treated every second he had with her as a precious gift with a limited supply.

He always thought they would live together until the end of their days and that they would defy the odds and die in each other's arms. Yes, it was crazy, wishful thinking to imagine that they would die at the exact same time holding on to each other like the embracing maidens of Pompeii. However, back then, he'd had no thoughts of her dying and leaving him all alone. Therefore, anytime he thought about death, which he hardly ever did, although he knew it was inevitable, he thought about an idyllic passing that involved the two of them together in the afterlife.

Not in a million years could he ever have imagined that she would die before him or that she would die when they still had so much of their lives ahead of them. She was the healthier person, the one who worked out more, who ate right, and she kept every appointment with the doctor. He was the brute who ate anything at any time and always found it insanely difficult to keep his appointments with his doctors.

She was always pushing him to stay fit and to keep up during their morning runs. He preferred to lift weights and train his muscles. She was also the one pushing him to keep his appointments with the doctor and to eat more fruits and vegetables. By all standards, he should have died first. If there was a god, and that god had the slightest clue what it meant to be fair and just, Mia never would have died so early, and she sure as hell wouldn't have died before him.

Michael chuckled as he imagined what Mia would think if she heard his thoughts. She would have scolded him for being blasphemous, and he would have laughed it off, almost exactly as he chuckled now.

He walked to his desk and switched on his gaming computer. He waited for the system to boot up before clicking on the writing software he had installed. He opened the only document he had saved and stared at the blank page like he had done for the past six months. He'd written nothing. He'd spent all that time thinking. A friend of his had told him to write down his thoughts so he could deal with his grief. It had sounded like a good idea initially.

Writing down his thoughts and turning them into something productive seemed like a healthy way to heal. However, after a few months of simply staring at a blank, white page, he began to come to terms with the fact that he was never going to write anything. Nevertheless, he continued booting up his computer and staring at the page.

He'd realized that simply staring at the blank page and thinking about Mia had become one of the best parts of his day. Merely thinking about what to write without even writing a single word was enough to send his mind down memory lane to a time when life was simple and happy and good.

As he stared at the blank page, his mind drifted and then went ahead to wander, searching for the perfect memory to fit the moment. Finally, his mind settled on the memory of them walking Roxy together. The most mundane memories were always the most emotional for Michael. Memories of their wedding day or their many anniversaries were over the top and were always playing in his head. They were easy to find, mainly because they were documented with pictures that had been gently and carefully placed in albums and frames.

However, the simple memories, like wrapping his arms around her while she did the dishes or watching her trying to learn how to play video games and failing miserably, were the memories that brought tears to Michael's eyes. Those memories reminded Michael that even the simplest of moments with Mia had been absolutely perfect.

He saw himself walking through the streets of their suburban neighborhood with Mia wrapped around his arm. She'd dug her face into his upper arm, barely even paying attention to the path they were on as she'd savored the smell of his cologne. Michael played his part in the sublime scene to perfection, staring ahead like a brave knight with his damsel wrapped around his arm. Bouncing around in a circle around their feet was Roxy. The way she jumped around, running ahead and running back, created an elegant contrast to the solemn grace with which Michael and Mia walked.

Michael found it sad that he always saw these memories from the perspective of a third person, almost as if he were not a part of the memory but only a mere onlooker. It truly drove home the fact that she was gone and that her essence was slowly drifting away even though memories of her remained vivid in his mind. It didn't matter if he could see her clearly.

She had been gone for so long that she was now far away from him. He couldn't touch her or feel her even in his memories. He longed for the feeling of her wrapped around his arm while he looked straight ahead guiding them along the path called life. Hell, he longed for any form of touch from her, even if it was a mere breath blown across her lips.

But she was gone, and along with her went every opportunity he had to touch her and to be touched by her. Only the man in his memories enjoyed the privilege of being with her, and he envied the lucky bastard. He wondered how he could take his place and, as thoughts of reuniting with her by any means necessary began to slip into his mind, he felt a wet sensation on the tips of his fingers.

He blinked rapidly as his mind was jerked out of the beautiful, comfortable memory and forced back into its painful reality. Looking down to see what had broken his trance, he saw Roxy nipping at his fingers.

He chuckled and played with her fur, petting her head leisurely. She ran toward a corner of the room and came back with a tennis ball in her mouth. She dropped it in his hand.

"You want to go for a walk?" Michael asked.

Roxy barked in reply, and Michael took that as a yes. He threw the ball so she could catch it. He knew she would want to play ball when they got to the park. He stood up as he let out a heavy sigh.

"Come on then," he said, walking up the steps of the basement. He picked up Roxy's leash and hung it around the back of his neck. She was so well-behaved that he didn't need to put her on a leash. There was also the fact that they lived in a calm, pet-friendly neighborhood. The chances of running into someone that would mind a dog not being on a leash were really low. However, as a rule, Michael always left home with Roxy's leash. He preferred being safe over being sorry.

As he stepped out into the cold air of the evening, he suddenly realized that he was once again on the sidewalk, the dog at his side, the wind at his heels, and a cold place next to him. The only missing piece was Mia. Unfortunately, she was the most important piece. "You okay, Dad?" a voice called out from nearby.

Michael turned to find Jack standing a few feet away from him. He wondered how long he had been standing frozen on the porch like a robot that had run out of power.

"I'm good, son," he replied. He looked ahead for a few seconds as silence descended between them. Roxy barked, and Michael looked down at her. "I'm taking Roxy for a walk. Do you want to come along?"

Jack replied with a few seconds of silence before shrugging. "I guess."

"Good," Michael said as he started walking out toward the sidewalk with Jack next to him and Roxy running circles around their feet.

CHAPTER 2

Lori sat in her office in front of her computer; however, she wasn't staring at it. Instead, she was staring at the screen of her phone. She had a chat box open, and she waited for a text she knew would never arrive. She had been waiting for weeks, and even though she knew her relationship with Ken was absolutely over, she couldn't help but open her phone and stare at his chat box for what felt like hours on end.

The last message she had sent just said "Hey." It was a desperate attempt to reach out, to give things another try. He hadn't even bothered to reply. As she stared at the three-letter word, she wondered if she had gone too far or not far enough. She wondered if saying more, perhaps apologizing and asking for a date, would get things back on track.

On the other hand, she wondered if her texting first after the painful things he had said to her was a terrible move on her part. Reaching out to him at all felt like she was letting herself down, betraying herself, and trying to reach out to someone who clearly didn't value her seemed like a foolish move.

And yet, she couldn't help but wonder if a little bit of pressure would get things back on track. "An apology perhaps?" she thought.

However, she wondered what she had to apologize for. She wasn't angry at him; she was angry at herself. She never should have reached out to him at all, let alone considered apologizing to him. Was she supposed to be sorry that he wanted a younger lady with a firmer body and fewer opinions? Or the fact that he'd had the guts to tell her how very little he valued the time they'd spent together?

She wondered if it would have been better if he had suddenly ghosted her. If he had suddenly vanished, she could have kept on guessing, trying to figure out what she did wrong, or even getting slightly worried that he had been kidnapped. Her boyfriend when she was in college had done that to her. He simply vanished without a trace. She later found out that he wasn't a student at her college at all; he was on campus just to hang out with his cousin for a month.

That ex had simply stopped picking up her calls or replying to her texts without any warnings. At the time, Lori thought he was the scum of the earth. However, now she wasn't so sure, as Ken made her realize that there are worse ways to end a relationship than sudden silence.

She scrolled up to his old messages and began to read the hurtful things he said to her before he finally dropped the bomb that it was over.

Ken: 6:44: First, I want to say that it's not you. It's me. I can't do this anymore.

Ken: 6:44: Damn. I'm not sure I'm making sense here. I don't want to be a jerk, but I think we want different things. Last night, I realized I am tired of arguing with you and having to prove my point at every corner. I shouldn't have to defend my opinions all the time. I thought it was me at first, and then I realized that I am perfectly fine. You are the problem. Now, don't get me wrong. You aren't a problem. You're just problematic, especially for someone like me. A high-value man like me just has different needs, and I don't think they're needs you can meet.

"Hey, girl," Jessica said, breaking into Lori's reading of Ken's self-esteem obliterating text. She looked up to see her best friend in the world glowing with the same subtle, natural glow that never seemed to leave her dark skin. Her purple-tipped hair was tied up in a tight ponytail that stood up in a shiny and lustrous bundle, while her brown eyes danced. She had gorgeous cheekbones and, when she smiled, her cheeks rose to an angle that was absolutely enchanting. Dressed in a warm, navy-blue skirt and a white shirt with a pair of black boots on her feet, she looked professional and classy in a style that only she could pull off flawlessly.

"Hey," Lori replied as she set her phone down, and Jessica sat across from her.

"What are you doing?" She glared at her.

"Um…" Jessica hummed, trying to think of a perfect lie. "Working," she said, deciding to go with the simplest lie possible.

"On your phone? No, you don't work on your phone. You're texting Ken again, aren't you?" She drummed her fingers impatiently on Lori's desk.

"No."

"Then what were you doing on your phone?"

She forced a self-deprecating grin to her lips. Dammit, she should have come up with a better lie. "What are you, a cop?"

"No, just a friend that knows you can do better than a grade A jerk who calls himself a high-value man." She drew air quotes with her fingertips. "Do you know what really kills me about that man?" She waited a beat, even though Lori knew she didn't really want a response. "It's the fact that he mislabels himself every damn time."

"I don't mean to be a jerk," Jessica said mimicking Ken's voice. "And then what does he do? He goes ahead and acts like a freaking jerk. And what's all that about being high-value? A king never has to announce himself as a king. Everyone knows. He doesn't need to say it."

"Jessica, I know you are trying to make me feel better, but it's really not working. Thanks for the effort though. But think about it. He might have a point."

"What do you mean by that?"

"I don't know. I think I'm just tired of going from one relationship to another. Perhaps it's time for me to look inward and maybe make a few changes."

"You are perfect exactly as you are, Lori."

"Am I, though? You're my friend, Jessica. You're supposed to tell me that I'm perfect. You wouldn't tell me differently."

"Oh, trust me, honey. I sure as hell would. But if you don't trust me, then maybe you should hear it from someone else."

Lori chuckled. "And who might this someone else be? Do you have someone on standby waiting for your cue to tell me that I am perfect?"

"No. Although, that isn't an absolutely bad idea. Perhaps someone telling you how awesome you are might just be what you need to get your confidence back."

"Yeah, right." Lori snorted out a laugh. "Hopefully, a man who actually loves me and genuinely believes I'm perfect."

"I can take you to meet a man who genuinely believes you're perfect, or he can at least authoritatively tell you if you aren't. Although, he most likely won't be able to fall in love with you, what with him being a clairvoyant and all."

"A clairvoyant?"

"Yes. He is kind of like a priest, but he's not a priest of an orthodox religion like Christianity or any of those commercialized faiths."

"I know what clairvoyants are, Jessica."

"Really?"

"Yeah. Fraudulent tricksters, that's what they are. Please tell me you haven't paid this man any money."

"Come on, Lori, don't be like that," Jessica pleaded. "You are way too closed-minded. You need to make some room for a bit of faith and a bit of belief. I mean, you believe in love, don't you?"

"Yes," Lori said, rolling her eyes.

"Well, some would call love magical, and I agree it is a magical feeling. And I firmly believe that, if you want something magical to happen to you, you have to call it to you by actually believing in it."

Lori snorted out a short laugh.

"What you just said is the most logical argument I have ever heard in defense of something absolutely illogical."

She grinned. "I will take that as a compliment."

"It was."

"So, are you going to give love a chance?"

"I have no problem with giving love a chance. I have given love numerous chances. It's your magician I'm skeptical about. Although, in retrospect, I think it's high time I started taking the idea of love with a pinch of salty doubt."

"Stop saying that. Love exists. Blake and I are living proof of its existence."

"Yes, Blake. I was wondering how long it would take for you to bring him up."

"Someone is getting jealous."

"God, no. Well, maybe. But not in an envious, spiteful way. More like the "happy for you and I hope to have what you have" way."

"Well, if you want to be happy like me, then my clairvoyant can help. He would lead you to what you want if, and only if, you have a little faith and give the universe a chance."

"Okay, please stop talking. My head feels like it's spinning. Walk me through how this man operates. Is he like a love guru who sets people up on dates? Or does he have a crystal ball with which he sees your soul and your soulmate?"

"Don't be coy, Lori."

"I'm not," Lori said as she let out a stifled chuckle. "I'm really not. I just want to get familiar with all the ridiculousness before I decide to walk right into it."

"Oh, stop it," Jessica warned. "You're lucky you have a friend like me who has a taste for your sense of humor. I knew you would laugh if I told you about the clairvoyant. That's why I didn't tell you about him before. Truth be told, he led me to Blake."

"Really?"

"Yes. I went to see him one beautiful Saturday evening, and he read my palm. He gave me a bit of advice and, two weeks later, I met Blake. And the rest, they say, is history. That history led me to my present, and now it will be my lovely future."

"Nobody says that."

"Such a skeptic… Just give the clairvoyant a chance. What do you have to lose?"

"My precious time."

"You mean the precious time you had no problem wasting as you stared at old messages from Ken?"

"Now, that's just low. Fine. When do you suggest we visit this clairvoyant of yours?"

"Right now," Jessica said with a shrug. "The sun is down, the workday is over, and the clairvoyant accepts walk-ins. There is no time better than the present."

"Really? You don't think we should wait until the weekend?"

"No. We do it now. I am not sure I'll be able to drag you there if I give you enough time to think things over and come up with reasons why we shouldn't go."

"Get me roped into your hocus-pocus before my brain kicks in. Excellent strategy," Lori said as she got up and picked up her purse. "Let's go."

"For real? Wow, that actually worked," Jessica said, springing to her feet with excitement.

"It shouldn't have," Lori muttered to herself.

"I would stop talking now," Jessica replied. "Let's go," she said excitedly as she slung her arm through Lori's and led the way out of the office. "Oh, this will be fun. Trust me. You won't regret this."

CHAPTER 3

WALKING WITH JACK AND ROXY WAS ABSOLUTELY PLEASANT. IT was very different from walking with Mia and Roxy. It wasn't terrible. In fact, Michael truly enjoyed the time he spent with his son. It was odd that they lived in the same house but, sometimes, they were so far apart that it was almost like they were miles away.

However, walking with his son, Michael felt closer to him and, in an indirect way, closer to Mia, since she was the woman who gave birth to him and was the only person in the world that loved the boy more than his father. Michael, Jack, and Roxy arrived at the park just as the sun began to descend from the sky, setting in preparation for its rise the following day.

The orange hue on the horizon cast a gentle glow on the autumn leaves of the park, and the breeze, unheated by the sun, sent a pleasant chill through the air, softly blowing over man, boy, and dog. Roxy's short fur swayed slightly under the influence of the breeze like the blades of grass that covered the park.

Michael called Roxy and showed her the ball before throwing it into the distance for her to fetch. As soon as he let go of the ball, Roxy bolted off, wagging her tail with excitement and running at top speed with determination. With the dog gone, Michael and Jack were left alone to face the silence between them.

On the walk to the park, they had both focused on just walking, and the silence had been slightly bearable. However, now that they were in the park, there was nothing for them to keep themselves busy with, and the silence was absolutely awkward.

The silence felt like torture and, eventually, Michael decided to fill it with words.

"So, how is school?"

"Fine," Jack replied curtly as Roxy came running back with the tennis ball in her mouth. Jack bent down, and Roxy ran to him. He grabbed the ball and tugged at it before she opened her mouth and finally let him have it. Jack threw it once again in the direction that Roxy had come from. The ball went high and far, way higher and farther than Michael had thrown it.

"That's a bit too far," Michael said as he looked down to signal to Roxy and stop her from going after the ball. However, it was too late. She was off, running after it even while it still flew through the air. "Roxy! Roxy!" Michael yelled, calling to her as she ran off. Unfortunately, she was too engrossed with chasing after the ball to listen to his call. Michael considered chasing after her but decided against it. She was a smart dog.

She was sure to find the ball and bring it back. And even if she didn't find the ball, she was smart enough to abandon her search and return. So rather than run after Roxy unnecessarily, he decided to take the opportunity to bond with his son.

He let out a sigh and looked around. His eyes fell upon a park bench a few feet behind them.

"Let's sit," he said, gesturing for Jack to come along as he walked to the bench. Jack followed, and father and son sat on the bench, each taking an edge so they could rest their elbows and sides on the handles of the chair.

"Anything special going on at school?"

"Nope," Jack said, bending down to pick a pebble from the ground and fiddling with it as he looked straight ahead.

The conversation was going nowhere. Michael decided that if he wanted to connect with his son, he needed to take a risk.

"Got a girlfriend?" Michael asked, shooting the words out rapidly.

"What?" Jack replied, apparently shocked by his question.

"A girlfriend. Do you have one?"

Jack let out a single, dry chuckle that was more like a playful scoff. "I used to. We broke up last month."

"Wait. What? I didn't even know you had a girlfriend in the first place."

"Yeah. We dated for about a year. Mom really liked her."

"Your mom knew you had a girlfriend?"

"Yeah. I told her everything immediately after we started dating."

That made sense, Michael thought to himself. Matters of the heart were always her department. "She was the best person to talk to about things like that. Hell, she was the best person to tell about everything."

"Yes, she was," Jack agreed in a calm, solemn voice.

They sat in silence for a few minutes as they both stared blankly ahead.

"I miss her, Dad," Jack finally said in a voice that was so low and gentle that it didn't sound like the teenage boy he had grown into. Instead, he sounded like a younger, more innocent version of himself.

"I miss her too, son. Sometimes, I feel like I don't know how to breathe without her telling me how to do it. I worry about you," Michael admitted.

"I can say the same about you, son. I hardly see you these days, and you seem to always be off somewhere. I don't want to be a helicopter father cramping your style but, sometimes, I get really worried. Where do you go? Do you hang out with your friends?"

"No. Not much. I go to the train tracks most of the time. It's the only part of this town that doesn't remind me of her. Everywhere else reminds me of her. Either we had been there together, or she had told me about it. The whole town feels like her, like home. And home isn't home without her, Dad."

"A hollowed-out shell," Michael replied with a sigh.

"I couldn't have described it better," Jack replied. "So, I stay at the railway tracks and try to keep my mind as far away from her as I can."

"Does it work?"

"It used to. Not anymore. But it's not so bad. I'm getting better, I guess. And I believe that you are too."

"I am," Michael agreed. "I know we'll be fine in the end. But we have to stick together, Jack. We need to be there for each other. Don't hesitate to ask me for anything or to tell me about those things that you used to tell her. I might not be able to give you the kind of advice that she used to give, but I promise you that I'll listen and try my best to understand."

Jack smiled. "Luckily for you, I'm almost all grown up. You only have to hang in there for the final lap," he said jokingly.

"Yep. One final lap and you'll be off to college. Then I will be alone until you finally decide to throw me into a nursing home so I can slowly wither away."'

Jack laughed, a short and controlled double burst of amusement.

"But, seriously though," he continued, after a short pause, "I would never abandon you, Dad. And when I'm in college, you won't be alone. Roxy will keep you company."

Speaking of Roxy made Michael search the distance for her. She should have been back by now.

Jack also stood up and began to look around. "I must have thrown the ball too far, and she got lost. I'm so sorry, Dad."

"You didn't mean to," Michael said. "Let's just focus on getting her back," he added as he started walking toward the thick woods where Jack had thrown the ball.

CHAPTER 4

Lori wondered what she was going to say when she met the clairvoyant. She tried to imagine the kinds of questions he would ask so she could prepare herself for the answers she would give him. The entire experience was sure to be weird and uncomfortable. She couldn't help but worry that she would flip out and react in a manner that she would regret.

Lori had a lot of defense mechanisms she'd cultivated through the years that she unleashed anytime she felt cornered. And, as much as she wanted to keep an open mind and be polite, she couldn't help but suspect that, in the middle of the meeting with the clairvoyant, she would either get really defensive or bust out laughing.

Jessica made a right turn, and Lori found herself being driven down a road she had never driven down before. She knew she was still in Firestone, but she couldn't recognize any of the buildings around her. Unlike the buildings she was used to seeing in the gentle suburbs, which were beautiful bungalows with gentle lawns, the buildings on this street were tall and seemed to be designed to be affordable. On both sides of the street were rows of apartment buildings that had at least ten floors each.

"Um, Jessica, what are we doing here?" Lori asked as she realized that Jessica was slowing down and bringing the car to a halt.

"What do you mean? We're here to see the clairvoyant."

"Your clairvoyant lives here?"

"Yup. Oh, don't let the neighborhood scare you. It's perfectly safe. All the people here are poor, but they're not dangerous. Besides, even if they were, they wouldn't dare steal from patrons of their neighborhood clairvoyant."

"If he is so great, and he can see the future, then why can't he lead these people to wealth? Or at least lead himself to wealth and get himself out of this place."

"Okay, you are going to have to drop that mindset before we go in."

"What mindset? Would you like for me to stop using my mind?"

"If that would help you to give the clairvoyant a chance, then yes, I would like you to stop using your mind. What Blake and I have is perfect. Sometimes I think I'm living in a dream."

"I have met him, Jessica. And, I agree, he is perfect for you. I see you guys together, and it looks like you are both in paradise. He complements you. Your energies, styles, and even interests match. I think you guys were made for one another."

"Exactly. Sometimes I'm with him, and I can't believe how lucky I am. It's so easy. My former relationships were always a struggle. Dates were boring, the moments alone were awkward, and the arguments were soul-draining. But with Blake, it's all so easy. It's almost like our relationship is on auto-pilot."

"You have a great relationship, Jessica. I am truly happy for you. But I don't see the point you're trying to make."

"The point I'm trying to make is that Blake is my destiny, and I might have missed him if I didn't meet the clairvoyant."

"That makes no sense. The entire point of destiny is that you can't miss it."

Jessica rolled her eyes and let out a frustrated sigh.

"You know what? I'm done. Let's just go upstairs. You listen to the clairvoyant and ask him any questions that weigh on your mind. He is in a better position to explain everything to you," Jessica said as she got out of the car.

"Tired of playing clairvoyant's advocate?" Lori said jokingly as she also got out of the car and followed Jessica, who was already walking briskly toward the building.

"You're lucky I love you. Heaven knows that for anyone else I would have simply given up and let you go home to your empty apartment, wondering if you should text Ken."

"Ouch," Lori said with a wince. "Now that's just low."

"I'm sorry," Jessica said, turning to Lori, scared she had hurt her.

"It's fine," Lori said as she tried to shake it off. "You're right. I am already here. The best I can do is to take this entire experience seriously and get the best out of it."

"That's the spirit."

"Fingers crossed," Lori said as they both entered the apartment building. The walls of the apartment building looked dilapidated with paint peeling off and watermarks dotting the ceiling. However, as bad as the building looked, it didn't harbor any unpleasant smells. The lobby of the building smelled like nothing and, as they went up the stairs, the stairwell began to smell like flowers. Jessica didn't stop on the second floor or the third, nor did she stop on the fourth or fifth. She kept climbing the steps, leaving Lori guessing until they were on the tenth floor, and only then did she start walking down the hallway rather than continuing her ascent up the stairs.

Lori was happy that the climb was over and slowed down long enough to catch her breath. As they walked down the hall, she noticed a strange-looking door at the far end of the hallway. The door was very different from the other doors in the apartment building. Unlike the other doors in the building, which were green with gold-colored numbers, the door at the end of the hallway was red with its number written in chalk. Lori saw a white, almost translucent, fog seeping out from the space beneath the door, and she blinked twice, hoping that it was all in her head.

However, it wasn't, and no matter how many times she blinked, she still saw the fog seeping out in cloud-like puffs. She hoped and prayed that the door she was staring at wasn't the door Jessica was leading her to. However, her hopes were dashed as Jessica passed all the doors on both sides of the hallway and stopped at the ominous-looking door.

Jessica knocked twice, paused, and knocked twice again. A second later, the door swung open, and standing before them was a man with a dot of jewelry right in the middle of his forehead and a red toga wrapped around his body. His face was wrinkled like a shriveled raisin while his hair was nothing more than a sparse tuft at the back of his head tied into a ponytail. Overall, he looked skinny, old, and frail, but his smile was vibrant and energetic, especially when he smiled and revealed a mouth full of perfectly white teeth, which were in direct contrast to the rest of his aged self.

"Jessica, my love. Come in. I see you brought a friend," the clairvoyant said in a clear, rich voice as he stepped aside for his guests to walk in.

Jessica walked in, and Lori followed tentatively. As she stepped into the living room of the tiny apartment, her eyes ran across the entire room taking it all in at once. From the middle of the living room, she could see most of the one-bedroom apartment. She could see the kitchen, which also served as a dining room with its cute stove, oven, fridge, and a tiny round table. There was a closed door on the left side of the kitchen, and Jessica concluded that the door led to the bedroom.

Contrary to her expectation of an ominous-looking apartment with birds' feet hanging from the ceiling and voodoo dolls lying in the corner, the clairvoyant's apartment was clean and simple. The only weird thing was an incense burner on the tiny, round table that was in the middle of the kitchen.

The living room reminded her of her grandfather's house. At the edge of the room sat a set of couches and a small, flat-screen television. A short-bladed fan hung from the ceiling, and an air conditioner took up a corner of the wall, making a terrible noise even though it didn't seem to be doing much of its primary function of blowing cold air. At the center of the living room was a coffee table with absolutely nothing on it. The apartment was tiny, and it would have felt stuffy if it didn't look so very empty.

"Please, sit down," the clairvoyant said gesturing to the long couch as he sat on the single chair next to it.

Jessica and Lori sat down and waited for the clairvoyant to get comfortable and address them. It took a while for the clairvoyant to adjust his garments and settle into his seated position.

"Jessica," he said finally in a gentle, fatherly tone. "How have you been?"

"I am doing fine, Greg," Jessica said.

Lori found this very strange. A clairvoyant named Greg. It seemed like such a conventional name for a supposedly spiritual man. His name ruined the mood that Lori was really struggling to get into. As an afterthought, she realized that Jessica had probably intentionally avoided mentioning the clairvoyant's name because she didn't want her to judge him or his gift, and the fact that the two didn't fit together, before he could even begin.

"How is Ken? I take it that he is making you as happy as you deserve to be."

"He is. He is making me even happier than I feel that I deserve. Sometimes I feel like I'm in a dream, and the fear of waking up sends me into a terrifying panic."

"Don't worry, dear," Greg said. "You'll get used to being happy, and you'll finally be at peace with being at peace. After spending a large part of your life shoving your own destiny out of your reach, sometimes even fighting against it, the peace of finally following your truest path can be unsettling. But fear not. It is just your survival instincts kicking in. When your subconscious finally realizes that your soul is at peace and at home, your heart will settle down and your worries will vanish." He snapped his fingers, which made Lori jump.

Jessica nodded solemnly in agreement, even closing her eyes as she ruminated over the clairvoyant's words. Lori was left to wonder if she was just being crazy or if there was some sense to the words that came out of Greg's lips. To her, all he had said sounded like some absurd silly fiction. However, seeing how engrossed in Greg's words her friend was made her think twice.

"So, you brought your friend to see me. Why?" Greg asked.

"Aren't you supposed to know that?" Lori asked, unable to hold her tongue.

Jessica shot her a fiercely angry look that seemed capable of burning a hole through Lori's skull.

"Sorry," Lori mouthed to Jessica.

"Not a believer, I see," Greg said with a warm smile that did a good job of breaking through most of Lori's defenses.

The clairvoyant rose to his feet and stared at Lori.

"Follow me," he said and walked toward the dining area. He sat at the table and signaled for Lori to sit across from him.

"Would you like for me to tell you what you want to hear? Would that make it easier for you to believe?"

"Not particularly, but it would help."

"Good. Would you also like me to tell you what you ate for breakfast, the names of your parents, the year you were born, and the very hour?" he asked.

"Um..." Lori muttered, beginning to suspect that the clairvoyant was pulling her leg.

"I can answer all your questions. I can tell you everything about you. But it won't help. You will always find a way to explain everything I say or do. I could tell you everything about you, and you will say that I made a lucky guess or that Jessica told me all about you before you arrived. In the end, the specifics of what you came here for don't matter. Everyone comes to me for one thing and one thing only. They want to be happy. Happiness is the goal that their hearts desire. Sometimes they have a road map of how to get there but, more often than not, they took a wrong turn along the way. You, for example, think a good relationship like Jessica has would make you happy."

Lori's jaw dropped, but the clairvoyant continued without pause.

"You think a man would fit seamlessly into your life and make you the happiest woman on earth. That is the road map you have drawn toward your happiness. And, to be honest, your mental map has been poorly drawn. A man can't make you happy, Lori."

Lori fought the urge to get up and leave. She couldn't believe her ears. She hadn't told him her name, and Jessica couldn't have either. It was also obvious that he didn't know her name when he'd first laid eyes on her. And yet he had simply said it in passing as if it was something he was supposed to know, as though they had known each other for ages. It was after recovering from the shock of the clairvoyant dropping her name like a bomb that the shock of his statement hit.

"What do you mean when you say that a man can't make me happy?" Lori asked, getting defensive despite herself.

"I mean a man can't be responsible for your happiness, or at least not solely, and he sure as hell can't come into your life while you're like this."

"Like what?" Lori said, feeling insulted.

"On edge. I have barely said a few words and you're boiling over with hot anger. There are so many emotions blocking the normal flow of your life force. You are like a tight string, made to vibrate by even the slightest touch. A tight string can't flow with changes or wrap around new things. You need to find a way to eliminate the tension clogging up your soul. Tell me, what is the one thing that you can get that would improve the quality of your life and give you some level of peace and joy? I can sense that this thing is something you have always wanted, but you have refused to get it because you're scared of the responsibility and worried that it will hold you back from finding love."

As Greg's words flowed into Lori's ears, one thought appeared in her mind, and she immediately understood what the clairvoyant was talking about. "A dog," Lori said as she began to feel a wet warmth rolling down her cheek. It felt like tears, but she couldn't believe it.

She never cried. "I've always wanted a dog. But I never got one. There was always a reason to not get one. At first, I didn't have enough money to take care of a dog. Then I got too busy, and I felt as though I didn't have enough time. And then I got scared that I might meet someone who I really liked and vice versa, but the person wouldn't be a dog person, and I would have to choose between him and my dog."

"You do realize that you are barring yourself from feeling happiness with your own worries, correct?" He waited only a beat. "Mark Twain once said, 'I have had many worries in my life, most of which never happened.' Think about it. How many times have your thoughts and worries stopped you from doing the things that your heart desired even though they were perfectly harmless?"

"Countless," Lori said, sobbing despite all her attempts to control herself.

"And don't you think it's time you stopped listening to the voice of worry and start listening to the voice of your heart."

Lori found herself nodding in agreement like Jessica had been nodding earlier.

"Get the dog, Lori. Let that be your first step toward following your heart. Once you are on that path, you will quickly arrive at your destination. Or happiness. Whichever comes first."

The clairvoyant got to his feet and helped Lori up. He then gave her a long hug and let her sob into his clothes. He smelt like incense and flowers, and Lori took in the scents as her tears soaked into his toga. She didn't understand why she was crying so much. It made no sense. A bit of her began to suspect that there was something in the incense lamp. However, rather than listening to the cynic in her head, she shut the voice out and settled into the moment, experiencing it and letting her emotions flow without any hindrances. The feeling was liberating.

CHAPTER 5

THE SEARCH FOR ROXY LASTED ALL NIGHT BUT YIELDED NO results. The next day Michael had to go to work, and Jack had to go to school. However, come evening, they both met back at the house and resumed their search. They hadn't even planned to search together; it was an unspoken agreement. And then, for the rest of the week, they spent every evening searching for Roxy from sunset until nightfall.

However, at the end of the week, it became absolutely clear that their search was futile. They had posted fliers, reported her absence to the animal shelters, and they'd even searched the internet for clues on how to find a lost dog. One site recommended getting a search dog to track the missing canine, and they were still considering that idea.

Eventually, Michael and Jack began to consider the possibility that Roxy was gone for good. However, just as they were about to give up, a glimmer of hope appeared. Jack was walking home from school one evening, feeling rather sad as he blamed himself for losing Roxy, even though his dad had made it clear it wasn't his fault.

A few blocks from home, he ran into a pretty girl with brown skin and beautiful black hair. She had blue braces on her teeth which made her look absolutely adorable when she smiled. He was so enamored by her beauty that he stopped when she approached. Still busy staring at her beautiful face and the way her lips moved when she spoke, he found it difficult to hear her words and only came back to himself when he realized that she was offering him a piece of paper. It was a flier for an animal rescue adoption event in the neighborhood.

Jack muttered a word of thanks and got on his way. He was a good distance away from her when it finally hit him. Roxy could have been rescued by the animal rescue group. They could have rescued her thinking she had been abandoned.

However, as he kept walking home, now faster as he was eager to get home and share his thoughts with his father, he began to wonder why they didn't call the number on her collar. However, this question was quickly answered when he realized that the number on the collar was his mom's, a number that was now inactive. They would have tried to reach out and failed.

With this realization, Jack started jogging home, and he soon burst into a full sprint. He was worried that they might be too late, and Roxy could have been adopted by someone else. The thought of losing her left a bitter taste in his mouth and fear in the pit of his stomach.

He got home to find his dad waiting for him on the front porch.

"Hey, son. What's up?"

"We need to go get Roxy."

"Yeah, about that. Maybe I should go searching today by myself. I wouldn't want our search to affect your schoolwork."

"No. We aren't going to search for her. I think we should check with this organization," Jack said as he showed him the flier. "Do you think they might have her, Dad?"

Michael considered what his son said for a few seconds.

"But she has a collar. They could have… Oh," he said as he winced. "Get in the car, Jack. I think you might be on to something," he said as he descended from the porch and started walking toward his car. They both got into Michael's SUV and drove toward the animal rescue facility's physical location.

CHAPTER 6

After her encounter with the clairvoyant, Lori was determined to get a dog. It had been her dream for so long, and now she had everything she needed to get it. She had the money, the spacious apartment, and the willingness to go for it. The money to cover a dog's expenses and the spacious apartment had been hers for quite a while.

All that was missing was boldness and determination, which she now also had. However, the next day after meeting the clairvoyant, Lori got overwhelmed with work, and she forgot to think about her plans to get a dog. The day after that, she carved out some time, but she soon realized that she had no idea where dogs were being sold or offered for adoption.

She scrolled through the internet and, after hours of research, she finally decided that she was going to get a rescue dog. She might even find a dog that needed her as much as she needed it.

The next step was deciding which animal rescue organization she wanted to adopt a dog from. The search took a few more hours before she finally found an organization that wasn't too far from her home. She considered going there immediately to check out which dogs were available. However, she looked up from her laptop and realized that the day was almost over. The animal shelter closed by six o'clock, and it was already seven.

The next day, Lori tried to get off work early to go to the animal shelter; however, she lost track of time. One minute it was 4:30 pm the next minute it was 6:45.

The next day, Lori began to feel down. If she couldn't find the time to get a dog, how was she going to find the time to care for it? She soon sunk back into her old ways of cynicism and doubt. She didn't even realize it until the end of the week. It was almost time to get off work, and the epiphany hit her like a truck. Without giving it another thought, she shut down her computer and walked out of her office.

"No more thinking. Just do it," she said to herself.

CHAPTER 7

Michael and Jack arrived just in time. They ran into the animal rescue with their hearts in their throats and let out a sigh of relief when they saw Roxy walking around in the middle of a group of dogs. As soon as she saw them, she started barking with excitement and wagging her tail, eager to run toward them but obstructed by the small cage that she and the other dogs were held in.

Michael and Jack were so overwhelmed with happiness that they froze. They started walking toward Roxy when they suddenly saw one of the animal caregivers walk toward the cage and open it. She led Roxy out, and Roxy ran toward them, super excited.

Michael and Jack stooped down and began to pet her fondly, happy to have her back. They were so engrossed in their reunion that they didn't notice a pretty woman standing in front of them until she spoke.

"Hello," Lori said with a polite smile on her face.

Michael looked up and was shocked to see an extremely beautiful woman standing before him. Her face was soft and warm and, most of all, she appeared to be kind. She had soft features and rosy cheeks, full sensual lips, and a slightly crooked nose. Her eyes were the color of the sea, and when she smiled, revealing her perfect white teeth, her face transformed from beautiful to goddess-like. She looked like an angel with her beautiful blond hair falling down over her shoulders, and her clear skin seemed to reflect all the light in the room as if it was made of silver.

She was dressed in a beautiful red pantsuit and a white button-down shirt. Despite the fact that she was wearing a suit, the perfect shape of her body was evident for Michael to see. Overall, she looked like a sexy boss with the face of an angel.

"Hello," Lori said again, and it was only then that Michael realized that she had been expecting a reply.

"Hi."

"I'm Lori," Lori said, introducing herself shyly as she tried to remain composed in the presence of the tall, handsome man in front of her. His jet-black hair was cut in a low fade, making him look like a soldier. However, given his height, the massiveness of his arms and chest, as well as the breadth of his shoulders, he was a sight to behold. His deep, dark eyes looked kind, and, within them, Lori could see a wariness that he couldn't hide even when he put up a forced smile.

"Michael," Michael said.

"Like the archangel?"

"I don't think I would qualify as a member of the heavenly host."

"You surely have the build for it," Lori said before she could stop herself. She wasn't one to flirt so casually, but his effects on her were overwhelming.

"Um," Michael said, looking himself over as if he wasn't aware of what he looked like. He was feeling self-conscious. After a long and happy marriage with Mia, he hadn't even thought about how people saw him for a very long time. When he was younger, he'd been terrible at talking to women, and that was, apparently, still the case. Something about Lori and the way she looked at him made his heart reflexively flutter with excitement.

Lori began to feel guilty for making Michael uncomfortable and decided to state her reason for approaching him.

"It seems my dog likes you."

"Your dog?" Michael said as his eyebrows drew together.

"Yeah. I just adopted her," Lori said happily, unaware of the perturbed look on Michael's face. "Signed the papers and all. She is so cute. I just hope I'm able to take care of her and give her the home she deserves."

"She already has a home. With us," Jack informed her.

Lori was taken aback. "I don't understand."

The lady in charge of the animal shelter walked toward the trio.

"Hello. I'm Jenn," she said. "What seems to be the problem?"

"I don't understand," Lori said trying her best to be calm as she avoided jumping to conclusions. "There seems to be a mix-up."

"There is no mix-up," Jack said. "Roxy is ours."

"Apologies for my son's behavior," Michael said. "He is just a bit upset. However, he's right. The dog is ours. We have been searching for her for days now."

"Oh. I'm sorry about that," Jenn said. "We did find a collar around her neck with the name Roxy. However, we tried calling the number on her tag, but we couldn't reach anyone."

"Yes. The number belonged to my wife. "

"Oh. Did she change her number? You should have changed her collar to one with her new number on it."

"She didn't change her number," Michael said. " She died, and we forgot to change the number on the collar and tags."

"Oh," Jenn said, as she laid her hand on her chest. "I'm sorry." She turned to Lori. "I'm really sorry, ma'am, but it seems that the dog is theirs. I will collect their contact information in case any evidence comes up that counters their claim. But I doubt they are lying. Perhaps we can get you another dog? We have a handsome Labrador just like her in the back room. Would you like to see him?"

"Sure," Lori said happily.

"I'm sorry for the misunderstanding," Michael apologized. "I hope you find a dog that will make you truly happy."

"I hope so too," Lori said. "Fingers crossed," she added as she crossed her fingers and raised her hand for Michael to see. As she turned around to leave, Michael felt that he was letting a very big opportunity slip through his fingers. He mustered all the courage within himself and spoke.

"Um… this would be your first time getting a dog, right?" Michael said.

"Yes. Do you want to give me a few tips?" Lori asked with a smile.

"It would be an honor," Michael replied.

"Cool. Hopefully, I can find a dog I like who also likes me."

"Good luck," Michael said. "I'll be waiting outside," he added as he turned around to leave with Roxy and Jack in tow.

Outside the animal rescue shelter, Michael and Jack stood next to the car.

"Dad, do you like the woman we met in there?"

Michael held his tongue and tried to avoid the question with silence, but Jack was relentless.

"Dad."

"She was nice," he replied.

A moment of silence passed, and then Jack finally said, "I think she's cool. You should talk to her."

"What?" Michael said. "You think so?"

Jack nodded.

"Would you look at that? My son is giving me advice on women. Shouldn't this be the other way around?"

Jack chuckled. "Well, if it would make you feel better, the girl that gave me the flier to this place is right over there," Jack said as he nodded in that direction.

Michael turned and took a quick glance.

"Interesting. Then what are you doing here? Trying to ruin my chances?" Michael asked jokingly.

"No. I was trying to be your wingman."

Michael burst into a hearty laugh, laughing louder than he had in a very long while.

"I don't need a wingman, son. I can do fine on my own."

"Fine," Jack said. "But if you strike out just signal to me, and I'll try to salvage things," he added as he went off to talk to the girl.

Michael watched as his son approached the young lady with poise and tact, and he couldn't help but feel proud.

"Were you like that when you were young?"

"What?" Michael said with a jolt as he turned to look at the person hat had crept up on him. It was Lori.

"Sorry. I didn't mean to scare you. I got my dog," she said with excitement, looking down at a handsome young Labrador retriever that looked like a male version of Roxy. The two dogs soon sniffed each other until they built some level of trust and started playing.

"Seems like they are going to be good friends," Michael commented.

"I think so too," Lori agreed. "So, any tips?"

"Dogs are easy to care for. Feed them regularly. Dog food is cheap and easy to come by. Don't forget to give him a bath every now and then. And a regular appointment with a vet is also quite necessary. Oh, and walks. Don't forget walks. Every day. It's good for them and, truth be told, walking is my favorite part of the dog-owner experience."

"Hm," Lori hummed. "Thanks for the tips. I'll be sure to use them."

Michael nodded.

They stared at each other in awkward silence for a few seconds until Lori felt too uncomfortable and decided that standing in front of him like a fool was stupid. She had expected him to ask for her number or something, but he hadn't. She concluded that she had read him wrong.

"Well, then, I'll be on my way."

"Have a nice one," Michael said.

"And you too," she replied. She walked past him and toward her car. She was already thinking she should have pushed more when he spoke.

"Um...," he said nervously as he jogged to catch up to her. "I haven't done this in a really long while so forgive me for being out of practice. But do you want to grab a cup of coffee with me?"

"Sure," Lori said with a smile. "Tomorrow morning works for you?"

"Sure. We can meet here and grab a cup of coffee from the cafe a few blocks away. And bring your dog. We can walk them together. "

"That would be great."

"Have you named him yet?" Michael asked.

"Not yet. I'm still trying to decide on a name."
"How about we choose a name together tomorrow."
"That would be perfect," Lori said joyfully.
"See you tomorrow," Michael said.
"Bye," Lori replied and walked away feeling like she was on top of the world.

EPILOGUE

Michael sat in front of his computer thinking of what to write. It had been four months since he had met Lori, and things were going great. They took it slow, and she was very patient. With time, they began to fall deeper and deeper in love with each other. Michael quickly realized that Lori was a wonderful woman.

Beyond her beauty, her mind was absolutely engaging, and every conversation with her was an enlightening experience. Their minds seemed to operate on the same wavelength, and Michael soon found himself wanting to spend every moment with her. However, from time to time, he still missed his wife, and he knew that he would never stop missing her. Lori knew it too, and she didn't seem to mind.

He hunched over his keyboard and started typing.

Hello Mia,

I miss you so much. I thought writing my thoughts down would help, but I think that's ridiculous. This is a letter to you, and I hope the angels deliver it to you in heaven. After all, where else could you be other than the best place in existence.

There is so much that I would like to tell you, but I don't know where to start. Jack is graduating from high school next month. We wish you were here. I hope both of us can manage to make it through the whole ceremony without breaking into tears. I wouldn't count on it.

We used to joke about how we would finally have the time to go on vacations and have fun together with Jack out of the house. I remember all the plans we had for his room. We were going to set up a pool table and you were also going to start painting again. In all our plans, your death was never considered.

I miss you so much and, for a long while, I found it difficult to carry on. Jack struggled too. But now we are getting better, and I think it's all thanks to Roxy. She helped us to find a life that doesn't feel quite so empty.

No one on this planet can take your place in our hearts. You might be gone from this world, but you live on in our hearts and memories. And, thanks to Roxy, our lives don't have to feel loveless and empty. You always wanted me to be happy. That's why I am confident that you would be happy that I found love again.

I even have a feeling that, if you were here, you would be scolding me for taking too long. I love you, Mia, always and forever. And as crazy as it might sound, I am beginning to love Lori too. And her rescue dog, Charlie, of course.

Goodbye, Mia. I will send another letter soon. I promise.

SAVING MOXIE WITH HEART

CHAPTER 1

Marcus Haven locked his front door shut and shuffled the mug of coffee he was holding to the other hand so he could avoid dropping his freshly made lunch all over the ground. Brownie, his dark chocolate lab, would have loved the early morning snack, but he was already at the door ready to go to work. Marcus sighed, knowing he would have a long enough day at work because of last night's storm. He didn't have time for any mishaps. The storm had neared hurricane strength so the river was sure to be a mess and he, along with his staff, would have to check on each of the boats and their moorings.

The employees at the boat yard were already prepared for the early morning and longer-than-usual shift, as well as his promised lunch and sodas afterward. It was the least he could do for his hardworking staff after the summer's dramatic weather. The storms were constant, adding to the already suffocating humidity that clawed down Marcus's throat, but he made sure his staff members were properly fueled with a stocked fridge and bottled water throughout the property.

The rosy dawn greeted him as he started his truck and it rumbled to life, so gentle after nature's violence the day before. Brownie had jumped into the passenger seat with a furiously wagging tail, and Marcus had to keep the strong tail from knocking his coffee mug out of the holder or smacking him in the face. Marcus rubbed his ears before patting the steering wheel in gratitude that his truck didn't give him any problems this morning, as it usually did. Its mechanical heart must have sensed that today was not the day to mess with him and his bad mood.

The drive to work was the same as it had always been, with the exception of his faster speed in order to arrive at work sooner. There were few cops in Essex, one of Connecticut's smallest towns, and Marcus knew them all by name because they all had boats stored at the boat yard. Brownie kept his face out the window, inhaling the morning scents and tasting the wind. Marcus rubbed the dog's back, a smile tugging at his lips. This boy possessed the ability to alleviate early morning exhaustion.

Marcus pulled into the manager's parking spot three minutes and forty-three seconds later. He sighed in relief as the entire lot was empty. He didn't have enough coffee in his system to handle anyone else. He trudged to the administration office's side door and unlocked it before putting a door wedge in place for when the employees began to arrive.

Brownie sniffed around the parking lot at breakneck speed when he heard the wedge slide in. Marcus trusted his dog not to wander because their routine was always the same.

Marcus set about opening the offices while gulping coffee and bobbing his head to the classic rock station that echoed throughout the building, while Brownie checked to see if any staff were available to share their breakfasts, but there were none. The closing staff knew how much Marcus enjoyed started work to classic rock legends and kept it playing overnight after their closing time so he could open up to it. When he stepped outside, he had a small smile on his lips that quickly turned into a frown.

Despite the fact that it was still early in the morning, the humidity made the air feel drinkable rather than breathable, but it wasn't the heaviness of the air that made Marcus scowl. The debris from the storm's aftermath obstructed the path to where the boats were docked. He was supposed to check on the yachts and elite boats first in case of damage, and he wanted the answers before the owners flooded their phone lines with questions about their property. But that wouldn't be possible until all the river waste and tree limbs were removed, which would take him hours.

He found a nearby shovel, set down his coffee, and began clearing a shoulder-width path down the dock, spewing a slew of curses his mother would scoff at. Unfortunately for Marcus, the VIP section of the storage facility was down the longest stretch of dockway, but it did have a sturdy overhang that might have kept the majority of the storm debris out of the path.

Marcus shoveled the debris as quickly as he could and was past the first set of boats in twenty minutes. The water lapped against the boats and dock on either side of him, lulling him into a familiar pattern of ducking his body low with the shovel then arcing his arms to throw the junk into mounds on the dock's side. He and his crew took special care not to dump anything into the river. Not only was it bad for the ecosystem, but he preferred that customers not see the river as a swamp.

Brownie followed, sniffing at the docks as he ran down them. He was especially interested in the southeastern edge, and he whimpered softly, but Marcus ignored him in favor of the mess he was scooping away.

The first employee shouted at him when he was halfway down the dock, and it was his assistant manager, Arlene. "Where can I help?"

Brownie bolted toward the noise, his tail wagging furiously, and he barked at Arlene. She greeted him with a laugh and a treat in her hand.

Despite his muscles aching in protest, Marcus didn't break his working rhythm. "Make sure the paths to the showroom and office are clear, then come down here and help me clear this pathway!"

Arlene raised her thumb, and the older woman walked into the main building. Marcus sighed as the sound of more cars arriving at the employee parking lot reached his ears. He was looking forward to the arrival of the younger staff to assist him with the laborious tasks.

Brownie continued his sniffing duty around the boats and Marcus smiled.

Marcus had injured his back in a fishing accident last summer, and it hadn't been the same since. Any bout of cold weather brought on new aches, making this part of his job more difficult for his mid-thirties body.

His ex had always told him he needed to slow down his fast pace because he would get hurt if he kept going like this, but he never listened to her. Maybe that's why she'd abandoned him and Brownie five years ago, despite the fact that they'd raised a dog together. He had not heard from her since.

Marcus shook his head at the regurgitating thoughts that threatened to burst forth and returned his attention to the task at hand. His pace became angrier, and a smirk tugged at the corners of his lips. I'm not about to slow down any time soon.

Marcus peered inside the storage facility and counted the number of boats there. He could see no visible damage from his vantage point, so he exhaled a sigh of relief. He didn't have to spend a day arguing with Essex's entitled wealthy population. The pathway inside appeared to be filthy but it could easily be washed away with the power hose.

He was about to finish the last shovelful of dirt when he heard a faint splashing sound. He reasoned that it could be a fish or a branch falling from the overhead trees. Brownie whined toward the dock's edge and stared out at the river, his tail motionless.

Marcus rested the shovel against the wall of the overhead section containing the bobbing yachts when he heard the sound again. But this time it was accompanied by a faint whine. Could one of the boats be displaced and rubbing up against another?

Brownie barked and paced down the path. Brownie's ears perked up as he tried to figure out what was causing the whine.

Marcus turned on his heel, walked down the pathway he'd just carved out, and scanned each boat for their spacing and to see if any piece was hitting something else. His lab followed at his heels.

"Everything okay, boss?" A scruffy employee, Jack, peeked his head over a boat farther down the river as he was clearing away another section of the dock.

"I think my hearing is going. I heard a splash and a whine but I don't think it's any of the boats, and it's not Brownie."

"No, sir, I heard it too, but I think it's on the riverbank. Could be a fish or another critter trying to catch one." The shovel scraping against the dock continued, and Marcus admired Jack for his hard work. The young man was a constant stream of motion and was always willing to help anyone or stay later to get the job done. Marcus always kept an eye on him for a manager's position.

"Could be," Marcus muttered, but he continued surveying the area and found nothing of importance. From the balcony on the upper level of the building, he could see the riverbank better, plus he needed to grab trash bags to clean off the boats. He needed to see where everyone else was at cleaning, since they had less than an hour until they opened. "I'll be right back, Jack. Need water or anything?"

Jack's hair flopped as he shook his head, and Marcus turned toward the metal building at a light jog. There wasn't time to waste, and he checked his watch. Fifty-three minutes to go.

He climbed the wooden staircase to the left of the riverbank and dock, which led to an entrance. From there, he knew he would have the necessary height. Brownie was a giddy blur right beside him. Marcus scanned every part of the dock and riverbank for the source of the noise, but he found nothing. Marcus clenched his teeth at the inconvenient situation, but he'd make do with the trip up here.

"Is everything all right, Marcus?" Arlene strode out of the double glass door entrance, her hand shielding her eyes from the glare of the sun. Marcus felt the heat on the back of his neck and was glad he'd arrived early before the temperature rose.

Marcus frowned. "I keep hearing something down by the river, but I can't tell what." He shook his head and faced Arlene.

"We'll send one of the guys later to check out the bank for large pieces of litter. Maybe some boats crashed on the bank."

"Maybe. How's it going in there?" He jerked his chin toward the building.

Arlene began her speech about the property's status, but Marcus didn't hear her, not after hearing the faint splashing and the soft whine that followed. As he tilted his head toward it, the world fell silent. He expected to see only a flash of something black on the grass behind a thick tree base. Marcus took a step to the right, gripping the smooth handrail, to get a better look at what was below. He hoped it was just a flailing trash bag, but the whine didn't sound right. Sweat beaded on his brow that wasn't caused by the heat.

Noticing his owner's attention focused elsewhere, Brownie surveyed the area with his ears perked up, but he didn't seem to notice what was making the noise. Only Marcus saw it, but he couldn't distinguish what *it* was.

"What is it? What do you see?" Arlene's sharp question pierced Marcus's quiet bubble and he pointed at the black object.

"Do you see that black thing? What do you think it is?" He moved farther down the handrail until he was at the end of the balcony.

"Maybe a purse or bag or something. I'm not-" Arlene's answer ended in a sudden gasp at the same time Marcus saw an animal's head move past the tree. Even though Marcus was thirty feet from the creature, he could see perfectly the brightness in the animal's eyes.

Without a second thought, Marcus sprinted down the stairs and onto the path going along the river. His breath came in quick breaths and, within half a minute, he was next to the animal. Brownie had sprinted ahead and barked at the tree and the animal that lay there.

Within seconds of Marcus seeing the animal, he knew three facts. One, this was an enormous dog with dark fur. Two, he couldn't decide what breed the dog was by the amount of mud caked onto his body. The last one was the worst, and Marcus's stomach clenched at the signs of trauma marking this poor dog.

Blood pooled around the dog in the grass, and when Marcus knelt over the dog, he noticed its tail splashing in the water. It was probably expending all of its energy just to be heard in a last, desperate attempt to be saved. Its eyes were wide but exhausted as it looked up at Marcus, and it didn't try to attack him, even though such a reaction would be warranted, as much pain as it was in.

Marcus's eyes welled up with tears as he witnessed the display of trust, and he swallowed. He placed a hand on the dog's head and gently rubbed between its ears. The dog winced and remained tense, but did not move.

Brownie licked the other dog's face and let out a soft whine. His dark eyes flicked to Marcus's as if asking him what they were going to do.

Marcus gritted his teeth, determined to see that this dog lived. "Arlene!" he yelled and continued to pet the injured animal. "Please bring me a towel!"

Arlene sprinted toward Marcus with a beach towel in hand in less than a minute. Her gaze was drawn to the injured dog, and a sob escaped her lips. Marcus wrapped the massive dog up quickly after she thrust the towel into his hands.

"Please, go find me the best veterinarian in town and call me with directions."

Arlene sprinted off without another word to the office, and Marcus heaved the dog into his arms.

Jack rushed down the stairs as Marcus stepped away from the tree. Similar to Arlene's reaction, Jack's eyes went to the bleeding and muddy dog Marcus carried.

"Can you go ahead and start my truck and get the backseat cleared out so this big guy can come?" Marcus motioned to his belt, where his keys were clipped, and Jack nodded. "Please grab these from my waist and hurry."

Jack sprinted off, taking the stairs two at a time, and Brownie bolted along with him.

Marcus exhaled heavily at the sheer size of the dog. With all the grime on it, he couldn't tell what kind of dog it was, but he knew it was huge, and it was heavy. With the extra weight, the stairs were difficult, but Marcus focused on his breathing and pushed through. If this dog was still alive after the horrific trauma that it endured, then Marcus could make it to his truck. When he finally arrived at his truck, his arms trembled.

The passenger and back doors were both open, and upon closer inspection, the passenger-side front seat had been pushed all the way up to make room in the backseat. Marcus's tackle box, the one he used when he went fishing, which normally sat in the back seat, had been moved to the floor between the back and front seats.

Jack really deserved that promotion.

Jack settled the broken and battered dog into the back seat and closed the door. He ran round the front of the truck and climbed into his seat.

Marcus's phone rang as he sat in the driver's seat with Brownie next to him in the passenger seat, his gaze shifting from the open window to the whimpering dog in the back. He slammed the car into gear while holding his phone to his ear and sped out of the parking lot. "Where should I go?"

"Go to Marty's hardware store in town, and the vet's office is on the south side of the building." Arlene didn't skip a beat at his sharp question, already used to his gruff behavior.

"Many thanks, Arlene." Marcus hung up the phone. He hadn't expected her to respond so quickly, but she always tended to come through for him. He couldn't picture the vet's office and didn't recognize it, but it had to be the best, so he followed Arlene's instructions.

The drive into town would take five minutes, give or take, and he prayed there wouldn't be any patrol cars out as he pushed down on the gas pedal.

The dog let out a soft whine, and Marcus reached back to pet its massive head gently. "It'll be okay, bud. We're going to someone who can help you."

CHAPTER 2

IN LESS THAN FOUR MINUTES, MARCUS'S TRUCK SCREECHED INTO the veterinary office's parking space in the front. He honked the horn twice to let them know he was hurrying and slid out to heave the dog into his arms. The cloth backseats were coated in blood and dirt but that didn't matter as the dying dog whimpered in his grip. "Shh, we're here getting you help, okay?"

Brownie vaulted out of the truck as well and was immediately on Marcus's heels with his nose to the ground.

Shouldering the truck doors closed, he moved as quickly as he could to the door but he didn't know how he was going to open the double doors with the bloody heap in his arms. Fortunately, his needs were met when the right door flung open and a middle-aged woman motioned him through. Marcus rushed through without pausing.

The waiting lobby's warm lights and crisp air conditioning greeted Marcus. "Please, help him. I found him at work on a riverbank. I don't know what's happened to him but help him!"

The older woman maneuvered around him to knock on a door behind the reception desk.

Rage flared in Marcus's chest that he was being ignored. Why wasn't she answering? The woman began typing into her computer and didn't look his way to acknowledge him at all.

"Hello? Can you hear me? Can you not see this dog is obviously injured?" The dog whimpered again in his arms, causing his chest to cleave. He'd tear this building down if it meant getting them to listen and do something for this dog. Why was he the only one who rushed to assist this poor dog?

"My hearing is fine, and I don't want your loud tone to interfere with the recovery of our other patients." The receptionist didn't raise her head from her computer.

"Then do something! He's dying!" Marcus ignored her and yelled anyway. He almost felt bad when she winced, but the woman simply looked him up and down in slow motion, and then she went right back to looking at her computer.

Waves of rage flooded him and, if the dog hadn't been in his arms, he didn't know what he would have done.

A door clicked open, and a woman in her thirties with golden, shoulder-length hair strode out. She was dressed in a white medical coat and a peach blouse. Marcus would have thought she was lovely if it weren't for the scowl on her pretty lips and the glare in her blue eyes. "What exactly is going on?" She didn't direct her question at her receptionist, as Marcus believed she should have, but instead focused on Marcus.

Marcus cocked his chin to avoid her stare, but there was a fire in her eyes that he hadn't expected but begrudgingly respected. "The dog is dying." He cleared his throat as his voice cracked.

The vet just blinked and then finally said. "Apologize to her, and we'll get started."

Marcus spluttered. "Excuse me? You're going to deny service that can save an animal's life?" He couldn't believe what she was asking him to do. Did she not see the light draining from the dog's eyes? He did, and he was ready to throw up at the tragic sight. "How could you do something like that?"

The vet crossed her arms and didn't budge. "Treating my staff in a disrespectful manner will not get you anywhere. We serve the animals, not the humans."

Marcus curled his lip. "He's not my dog. Just treat him, dammit."

The vet was turning away when she asked, "Vinnie, will you give him a list of other vets in the area? I think the one across town is opening soon." What was she doing? How could she do this to an injured creature?

She was near the door when Marcus stepped forward, meeting the receptionist's eyes. "I'm... sorry. I shouldn't have spoken to you like that. Please help him." His teeth gritted as he muttered the apology, but there was a small smile on the receptionist's face.

"We will." Vinnie stood up and a whirlwind of activity began in the back office as she directed others to prepare the operating room and themselves for surgery. Everyone had forgotten about the dog that was still in Marcus's arms.

During the entire encounter, Brownie sat patiently at Marcus's feet, and his eyes volleyed between the talking humans.

Finally, a veterinarian technician came toward him with his arms stretched out and a question in his eyes. Marcus swallowed, and his limbs didn't move as he struggled to give the dog up. His arms stiffened, and he couldn't let go of the dog. Marcus could be done with this entire incident. He could go back to work and deal with the storm's aftermath, maybe get a call from Vinnie, then move on with his life. He could go down an easier road.

Marcus eventually passed the dog to the technician, and he could have sworn his heart cracked in two. He wondered if the technician heard the sound as Marcus let go.

The technician nodded and smiled down at the dog before striding to a room in the back office. Marcus tracked them until they were out of sight, but he couldn't loosen the breath stuck in his chest.

The vet was still by the door but hadn't gone in. Slowly, the woman turned and gave him her sternest look. "Your apology is appreciated. But if you ever come back, that attitude is not tolerated in my office, understand? But you can go. The dog will be taken care of to the best of our ability. If you want an update on whether he will live or die, leave your number with Vinnie." Then she left to follow the technician, and Marcus was left by himself in the waiting room staring after her. He forced his gaze not to drift too low.

He looked down at the blood crusting his uniform and skin. His mind went blank, and his body went on autopilot. Marcus felt his body move toward the door, open it for him and Brownie, and then walk to his truck. The door handles were smeared with brown flecks, and his stomach flipped. He peeked at the back seat through the window and his vision tunneled to the bloodstains.

Why wouldn't his body move? Why couldn't he leave? He should be able to walk away and go into stress mode at work to ensure that the facility was in working order. There was still so much to clean and be done but he *couldn't* move.

Marcus pulled out his phone and began dialing Arlene. She answered on the first ring. "You get there okay? Do they have him?"

Marcus didn't answer for a moment. Who would advocate for the dog? Where would he go since he'd washed up in the storm? The dog was big enough that shelters would think he was dangerous, so he would most likely be put down.

The decision that came to him was the hardest but the right one. "He's going into surgery now, and I'm going to wait here. I'll be off for the day so would you mind watching the store?"

Arlene sucked in a breath. "Yes, of course, boss. Glad the pupper is in good hands now. Give Brownie a scratch and treat for me." He knew she didn't mean just the "good hands" at the vet's office, and emotion clawed up Marcus's throat.

"Me too, Arlene, and I'll give him plenty. He's been a good and helpful boy today." He stopped, remembering that he'd promised the workers a lunch and sodas after their clean-up duties. "Can you do lunch for everybody by yourself."

He could almost hear her smile through the phone. "Of course, I can. Call if you need anything." Then he hung up. He strolled back into the lobby where Vinnie, now at her seat, perked her head up with a greeting on her lips.

"You're back."

"I'm waiting for my dog. I'm not going anywhere." He sat down on the plush seat and scanned the coffee table for anything interesting, but nothing drew his attention away from the crisis in front of him.

Brownie paced around the waiting room, sniffing every inch of the warm window with a tentative wag of his tail.

"Let me know if you need coffee or water. We have goodies reserved in the back for staff but you'll be here for a while. Also, we have dog treats for your puppy and dog food to buy, if you'd like. " Vinnie's eyes twinkled at him, then down at the chocolate lab, and Marcus looked away. He didn't deserve her kindness after the way he'd treated her.

Marcus clasped his hands in his lap and stared at the dirt caked onto his finger wrinkles. "I am really sorry for raising my voice at you. I was scared and haven't been in this position before. But I still shouldn't have taken that out on you. I'm sorry." He looked up to find her smirking.

"Arlene warned me about your grouchiness so don't worry, honey. There's no love lost between us." She winked and then went back to her computer.

At least there was that. Now he wondered how to combat this new worry with distractions. He didn't particularly enjoy scrolling on his phone and wished he had a book in the car.

For hours, he watched the news on the overhead television, and a couple of times he dozed off only to wake up to the sounds of doors opening. But it was only the technicians running around the back office, not the vet, who never came out.

While he was dozing off, Vinnie placed a hand on his shoulder and jolted him awake. Brownie shifted from his position on the floor, coiled into a tight ball, and propped his head up. She took a step back, as if he were a grizzly bear on the prowl. "I apologize for startling you."

He rubbed his face with one hand. "That's fine. Is there any news? Is he okay?"

"We don't have news yet. But we do know that he is actually a she."

Marcus raised his brows, certain that the dog was a boy based on its sheer size but, looking back, it could have been either. "Good to know. Thank you." He went back to closing his eyes when she cleared her throat.

"I was running out to grab lunch for Claire and wanted to see if you were hungry for anything."

Marcus reached for his wallet, only to realize he'd left it at the storage facility. His stomach gnawed at him, but he pretended not to feel it. "I'm not hungry, but I appreciate it." Vinnie's kindness surprised him after what he had done earlier that morning. His mama would have yelled at him; she would have been ashamed at how he'd treated a woman.

Vinnie clucked her tongue. "Nonsense. What do you want? I'm going out for subs."

"Nothing for me, thank you. Really."

But the older woman shook her head and went out the door, muttering softly, "You're just as hardheaded as she is."

CHAPTER 3

Marcus didn't know who Vinnie was talking about but he didn't care too much. He didn't think this trip through, and maybe he could convince Jack or Arlene to drop by with either his wallet or the lunch he'd stashed in his office.

Perhaps Vinnie would allow him to buy dog food and pay later or he'd have to take Brownie home. But Marcus needed the comfort of his dog in order to face this day.

Swarmed by his thoughts, he was startled at the vet meandering through the office in search of something. She was bedecked in soft blue scrubs with wagging dogs peppered along the sleeves. When she noticed him there, she stopped and her perfectly groomed brows raised. "You're still here."

Her disbelief made him bristle, but he knew it was well-deserved. Marcus's first impressions were usually not good. He splayed out his hands in a *what do you do* motion then replied, "Still here."

The vet cocked her head to study Marcus. "She won't be awake for hours. You and your pup should go home or it'll be a long day."

"So I've been told." He rubbed the back of his neck, and she was turning away when he blurted out, "Will she be okay?"

The vet chewed her lip. "It's hard to say. She sustained and suffered horrendous injuries for hours. The storm she weathered on a riverbank was a bad one." She shrugged her slight shoulders but there was exhaustion weighing them down. "I wish I knew how she'll fare, but we do know she's a fighter."

Emotion clogged his throat, but he cleared it before he spoke. "Thank you. It's incredible what you do."

"My name is Dr. Claire Lovery, and it's my honor to help animals." It sounded like a mantra she repeated every day.

Her name was beautiful, and when she wasn't glaring at him, she was even more stunning. But he had to admit to himself that he did love the sight of her glaring and angry at him. He hadn't encountered anyone who could stanch his anger in such a way, and he wondered how much fire she contained, if it burned as hot as his and how much more.

"I'm Marcus Haven. I work at the boat yard down the road." He wanted to shake her hand, but she was in sanitary garments, and she didn't come closer. But Claire smiled at him before she stepped back toward the operating room.

"It's nice to meet you, Marcus. I hope to see you around." Then she was gone after a quick smile at Brownie.

Marcus pursed his lips before a toothy grin spread across his face. Her name was lovely and suited her well. But her spirit was intoxicating, and he wanted to learn more.

Vinnie walked through the front door carrying a tray of coffees in one hand and a filled bag in the other. She appeared to struggle with the weight, and Marcus hopped up to lift the tray from her arms.

"Oh, dear, thank you! I don't know how I managed to get through the door!" Vinnie was flustered and settled her purse and the bag of what smelled like meat sandwiches on her desk.

Brownie jumped up in the interest of the delicious food, and his tail viciously swished. He trotted around the pair with his tongue out and bright eyes shining.

Marcus coughed to cover his grumbling stomach and set the coffees on the counter. "It's not a problem. It's the least I can do."

She gave him a bright smile before handing over one of the coffees and a sandwich she pulled out of the bag. "For you, dear. Go get comfy and change the channel to something you like. I won't be troubled, and the other customers won't either." Winking at the empty room, she kept her hand extended with the sandwich, but he couldn't take it.

"I don't have money on me, but thank you, really."

"Nonsense. Take it so we don't have to listen to your empty stomach anymore," she insisted but not unkindly.

"I'll bring my money tomorrow or have one of my employees bring my wallet later on." He hesitantly accepted the sub and coffee, and his stomach rumbled in response.

"I'm not worried. The only catch is I ordered what I would for our dear doctor, but enjoy! You have a long day ahead of you."

It occurred to him that Marcus didn't tell her his name and yet she'd bought him lunch. The guilt stewing in his stomach worsened, and he knew he'd have to make this up to her somehow. "My name is Marcus, by the way. Thank you for lunch. I really appreciate it."

Vinnie waved him away and began separating the food and coffees. "No worries, Marcus. Go eat while it is still hot."

For the first time, Marcus obeyed Vinnie, settled into the armchair, and unwrapped the sandwich. It smelled delightful, and he didn't examine it before he took his first bite. Flavors burst on his tongue at the breaded chicken, vegetables, and sauce mixing in his mouth. The doctor ordered this? Claire had good taste in food, Marcus admitted to himself. Perhaps he'd ask her what it was so he could order it for himself sometime.

Marcus sat in silence watching the latest weather report to see the fishing conditions for the next weekend. He wanted to go out with some buddies but, depending on the dog, he didn't know what he was going to do. But he watched anyway and kept a keen eye on the door that Claire would come out of.

His coffee and sub were long gone hours later when Claire clicked the operating room door shut. "I'm starved, Vinnie."

"Your food is in the fridge, sweetie." Vinnie had told Marcus she was doing the last of her closing list moments earlier. She had spent a significant part of the morning calling clients to inform them that they had an emergency and had to reschedule a few appointments. She didn't seem to get any complaints, and Marcus wondered about the reputation of this office. Everyone was so *nice*.

Claire opened her mouth to say something when she noticed Marcus sitting there. "You're still here."

Marcus smirked. "You keep saying that."

"I just thought you would be gone." She gave him a kind smile and surprised Marcus by leaning on the counter to eat her sandwich. "Tell me how you found her."

While Claire inhaled her food, Marcus told them the story, and he was surprised the vet could continue eating. Marcus's stomach roiled just remembering this morning. When he was finished, Claire was piling her trash into a ball, her mind whirling with her thoughts. Lost in thought, she was beautiful.

Marcus cleared his throat. "Can you tell me about the surgery and the dog's injuries?"

Vinnie and Claire shared a look before the latter faced Marcus with a clenched jaw. "The worst of it is over, but I still have work to do on her body. She just can't take anymore right now." Claire inhaled as if to soothe her temper, and Marcus cocked his head. He wasn't going to like what she said. "I won't go into detail, but if you're interested, I'll send you my report when it's finished."

The slight against Marcus stung, and he was shocked. He found he did care what happened to the dog and as Brownie looked up at him with pleading eyes, he reached down to scratch his ears. Marcus had a feeling his life was about to change.

"What are her worst injuries you have to fix?"

Claire blew out a breath and pushed back her bangs. "She had a lot of internal bleeding. We had to do a transfusion. Her lungs had water in them so we will worry about pneumonia setting in, and we repaired tears in her throat."

Marcus listened to the long list of injuries she continued to describe. With each item described, a stone struck his heart and filled his chest. His breath came out raspy and salt pricked his eyes. How had she survived?

Sensing Marcus's distress, Brownie plopped down onto his feet and peered up at Marcus patiently. Marcus dragged his hand through

Brownie's thick fur, and he found Claire's eyes following the movement.

They met eyes and, for a moment, the world quieted. Marcus's heart thundered as she opened her mouth before licking her lips. He was utterly transfixed by her.

Marcus shook himself and blinked. "How long will her recovery be?"

She cleared her throat. "It will be a long journey for her if she survives."

If.

The word clanged through him, and he struggled to believe there was a world where this dog with a fighter's spirit wouldn't survive. "If she survives?"

Brownie whimpered at Marcus's change of emotion but Claire wasn't fazed and reached for treats and handed one to Brownie. There was a soft smile on her lips as she looked at Brownie.

His tail wagged slightly at the treats, and he padded over to accept one. "There was a lot of damage and, if she survives, she'll need an owner to be extraordinarily patient and attentive to her needs. She could have a normal life with the right care."

Marcus hadn't thought about that, about the long recovery she'd have. Would she be in capable hands?

"She's mine. She'll be in good hands and will fit right in with Brownie." The words were out of his mouth before he even realized he'd spoken.

Claire's eyebrows lifted to her hairline, and guilt seared through him. Did he really come off that badly that he didn't seem the type to care for an animal? He didn't want to reflect too closely on that.

"You want to take ownership of a dog that has a one percent chance of survival?" Vinnie and Claire's eyes widened at him, and he only straightened.

"Yes. We're a family of survivors and, if she lasted through that storm and survived, then it's my honor to be her human."

The words hung in the air, and Claire's face softened. "The bills will be high, but we can find fundraisers and charities that can help."

"We could rally the town to help, and maybe we'll find out the previous owner's identity," Vinnie added and sipped on her coffee.

"I have some savings." Not a lot, but he did have some.

Claire nodded and a dark expression flickered over her face. "I have some pals in the force that might help, but I'll leave that to them. I should return to her to see how she's doing, and you should probably go home and get some rest."

Indeed, the sun had fallen over the horizon an hour ago, and he was craving dinner but didn't want to say anything. But out of everyone in the room, Claire had had the harder day, and she didn't seem inclined to leave anytime soon.

"I'll get us dinner if that's okay with you? Do you like barbecue?" Marcus rose and Brownie trailed after him in a sleepy daze.

Vinnie covered her mouth with a hand and made herself appear busy, but Marcus's eyes were on Claire. Amusement danced in her eyes and her lips tugged upward. "I am known to enjoy a pulled pork sandwich once in a while."

Marcus grinned. "I knew I had a good feeling about you." A blush crept up his cheeks as the words slipped out but he noticed she had rosy cheeks as well. "I'll be back in an hour with food." He scribbled his number on the pad waiting on the lobby table and patted his leg for Brownie to follow.

Claire picked up the number, and her smile grew. "See you in a bit."

CHAPTER 4

Marcus returned to Dr. Lovery's office in less than an hour with takeout boxes of steaming food in both hands. Dinner was the least he could provide after she'd saved the dog's life and dealt with his bad attitude this morning. He knocked on the glass and peered through to the dark lobby but a light turned on, and then Claire's familiar warmth appeared.

Claire's eyes found the bags of food first, and she grinned. The sight sent his heart racing but he shook himself. He had just met the woman and was already buying her dinner.

She's saving my new dog so I need to be grateful rather than looking for romance, he told himself but his heart didn't want to listen. She was staggeringly beautiful, even more so with her hair down.

The door opened, and a rush of air conditioning slammed into Marcus, in contrast to the humidity threatening to choke his airway. He hoped he didn't look like a sweaty mess, but it was too late now.

"Where's Brownie?" she asked as he slid through the entrance, and she locked it behind him.

Marcus shrugged. "He's sleeping in front of a fan. He's in a bit of a food coma after being spoiled from his long day."

A smile twitched on Claire's lips, and Marcus wanted to grin but tried to maintain his cool. "Brownie did have quite a rough day."

The joke almost passed through Marcus but her sly humor released his restrained grin. "Nice one. Who knew vets had a sense of humor?"

"Indeed, who knew?" she replied drily and led him to the back offices. She strolled through the door marked as hers and his expectation of a cramped closet that one would call an office was surpassed. Her office was openly laid out with a couch and a coffee table on one side, and her oak desk sat in front of a rectangular window. The desk was organized, as were the bookcases lining the opposite wall from the entrance.

Marcus let out a low whistle. "Your office is nice, Dr. Lovery." He set their meals on the coffee table, and he began sorting out the food.

The intoxicating smells gnawed at Marcus's stomach, and he refrained from jumping right into food without waiting for her. She shut down her computer before coming over.

"Thank you. I'm just glad it wasn't the size of a closet. When I was looking for a property, that seemed to be a common theme." She plopped onto the couch and dug into her food, without looking at Marcus. "Oh, my god. This is delicious. I feel like I haven't eaten in years."

Marcus suppressed his chuckle and marveled at her comfort with him already. She seemed completely at ease in his presence and even set her feet up on the table.

"My buddy, Charlie, owns a barbecue joint down the street, and he makes one of the best pulled pork sandwiches in the state," Marcus told her proudly.

"He must be one hell of a man to create something so delicious." Claire practically moaned, and a grin tugged at Marcus's lips again.

Marcus nodded. "How long have you been a veterinarian? What made you want to go into animal science?"

Claire dabbed at her mouth with a napkin as she gave him a funny look. "I've been a vet for nearly ten years. My uncle was one, and I loved to join him at his practice to help with the animals. I'd help walk the dogs or pet the cats or help his secretary with odd tasks." A smile formed as she remembered the past.

"Does he still practice?"

She shook her head. The motion pushed hair in front of her eyes, and he itched to brush it behind her ear but he stifled the temptation. "No, he's enjoying retirement in Arizona but he taught me a lot before and after school. I couldn't have done it without him."

"He sounds nice. I'm glad he could do that for you. Do your parents live around town?"

Claire raised her eyebrows. "These are sounding like first date questions."

He shrugged and leaned back in his chair. "Just two people eating the best pulled pork sandwich in Connecticut and discussing their lives. That can be all it is."

"Seems like a first date."

Marcus smirked. "Do you want it to be our first date? I have a dozen other ideas I'd like to do with you that would be considered a first date, not a dinner at your office like an old married couple. This sort of encounter would be down the road, not day two of knowing each other."

She grinned. "Now we're an old married couple?"

"Are you considering this a date?" His eyes pierced into hers, and a blush crept up her cheeks.

Claire Lovery stuttered and looked away, anywhere he wasn't, but she couldn't form the words needed to reply. "We're eating a meal. That's all."

"For now."

She coughed. "Are you saying there will be another time?"

He smirked. "If you'd like to. I would. I find you to be brilliant and fierce and caring. But best of all, you can handle my rugged appeal better than most people I know."

Her eyebrows rose even further before she snorted. "You call that nasty attitude rugged appeal?"

"Hey! I have a heart of gold once you get past the gruffness." He raised his hands as if to ward off whatever she was about to retort even though he knew she probably would anyway.

"Must go through a thick layer to get to the heart of gold." But she winked, and both of their smiles grew.

He finished his pulled pork and crumpled the wrapper into the bag. He didn't want the night to end, and part of him wondered if she felt the same. "You must have older brothers. There's no other way you're this tough."

She shook her head. "I'm the only girl in a family of tough men. Softness wasn't exactly encouraged."

The thought sobered Marcus, and his grin faded. "Pretty tough growing up then?"

But her grin spread, and she tossed her trash into the bag. "It was an eventful childhood but not rough in the slightest. There are perks to being the only woman in the family." She gave him a pointed look. "I have a lot of gun-toting uncles and cousins who are very protective of me." She stood up and disappointment coursed through Marcus at their night coming to a close. But Claire gestured to the couch, and she slipped off her shoes before throwing herself into the cushions.

Marcus quirked a brow at her casualness but didn't say anything and instead followed behind. "Thank goodness, I know a few food joints that can make you happy."

Pinkness stained her ears, and she looked down. "Food is the way to my heart."

Thank goodness he'd started with an easy meal. Claire deserved a high-end restaurant, and Marcus realized he wanted to accompany her to one. Marcus got comfortable on the couch and let out a deep sigh. His stomach was filled with the good food and his heart was brimming with the presence of the good woman in front of him.

"What about your family, Marcus? What are they like?"

"I have just my brother and my parents. My uncle lives in California with his sons, so it's just us. We get together on Sundays for dinner." A wash of emotion fell over Marcus. He wanted to tell her everything, and he had to refrain from spilling his soul into her stunning blue eyes. What was going on with him? He'd only known this woman for hours.

Claire cocked her head and tucked her feet under her legs. "Does your brother have kids?"

Marcus smiled. "He has a daughter, Emily, and she is the center of the family. That girl is spoiled rotten, but she's amazing. Plays softball, too."

"Must be nice to dote on a child. I've always wanted my siblings to have kids so I can have nieces or nephews," Claire sighed.

Marcus's smile slipped into a frown. A daring question tickled his tongue, and he wasn't sure if it would be too forward but something in the way they were connecting made him think it would be suitable to ask. "Do you want your own kids?"

Shock rippled across her face, and she shifted in her seat. "Quite a first date question. I've never met someone so forward."

Marcus smirked. "So this is a date?"

Redness spread on her cheeks, and she waved him away. "Just a meal, Marcus. I operated on your new dog and, for that, you owe me dinner. And for your poor attitude."

Lifting his hands, Marcus's mouth twitched. "You're right. I know it's just a meal but I'm a curious and forward man. I like to know who I'm sharing a meal with." He gave her a pointed look.

The silence was deafening between them, and Marcus wondered if he'd made the wrong choice in asking that. He picked at his nails and was on the third when she finally answered. "I would like my own but I haven't met the right person to have children with. I was contemplating doing it myself in the next few years if I don't meet anyone."

Marcus gave her a soft smile. "Let's hope you've met the right person for such an honor."

An unexplainable emotion flashed across her face, one he couldn't distinguish before it was gone. Silence filled the room, and he knew that part of the conversation was over so he searched for a new topic to broach, one that was safer to discuss. "Was your uncle the reason you wanted to get into animal services?" Marcus got comfortable next to her again and struggled to face her. Her beauty was mesmerizing, and he didn't want to blubber in front of her.

Claire sighed before a small smile appeared. "Sort of. I've always loved animals and taking care of them. They're easier to work with than dealing with people."

Marcus laughed. "Humans are a different kind of breed, so I understand it."

The smooth conversation flowed into the early hours of the night each smiling and animated as they broached every topic. Neither saw the clock as it passed midnight and then one in the morning. It was the alarm on Dr. Lovery's phone to check ion Marcus's dog that popped their bubble.

"Crap, I need to check on her." The last word ended with a yawn, and Marcus checked his watch.

"Wow, I didn't realize the time. I should probably get home. Brownie will be worried."

They both rose from the couch, their bodies groaning at sitting in the same spot for hours but neither seemed inclined to leave the other.

"When can I see you again?" Marcus shoved his hands in his pockets.

Claire smiled. "Won't you check on your new dog tomorrow?"

"Well, yes, but I mean out of the professional scope. I'd like to take you to dinner. I've enjoyed myself tonight, and getting to know you has been a pleasure I'd like to continue." He could have sworn a blush crept onto her cheeks but, in the dim light, he couldn't be sure.

"I'm free tomorrow night. Pick me up here at seven and show me another delicious spot you enjoy."

Marcus's heart soared at her answer and, after their incredible evening that ended too soon, he knew he wanted more time with her. He was fascinated by her life and views, and he was mentally counting down the hours until he would see her again.

He grinned. "Sounds like a date."

The pair checked in on Marcus's dog before Claire walked with him out to the parking lot.

"Tonight was actually nice, Marcus. Thank you for dinner and a pleasant conversation. You're not as bad as your first impression made you out to be." Her dry tone would normally grate on Marcus's nerves but ,despite his heavy eyes, a grin bloomed on his lips. "It was a delightful evening, and I'm glad my gruffness doesn't bother you."

Claire left him at his truck with a wink, and he thought about her as he drove home, and then he met her beautiful face in his dreams.

CHAPTER 5

Marcus changed the plans, albeit slightly, and he hoped Claire wouldn't mind. After their remarkable evening last night, he didn't want to do the typical dinner. She deserved more than a night so mundane.

When he checked in on his new dog, the name for her came to him. She would be called Moxie after the trauma she'd suffered through and survived. He shared the name with Claire, and her eyes glowed when she heard it.

"The name is very fitting. Brownie will have an incredible sister to admire."

Marcus agreed and couldn't wait to make her collar, her badge of survival.

He told Claire where to meet and dropped off a coffee to Vinnie as an apology for the previous day.

The older woman smiled into her mug during the visit and waved goodbye with a twinkle in her eyes.

Marcus was waiting for Claire at half-past six at a boat dock a mile south of the boat yard. His hands were clammy as they held the bouquet, and he tugged at his suit. Never had he made this much effort, but he couldn't pass up this special opportunity.

Claire didn't leave his mind all day and, on numerous occasions, his staff had to snap him out of his daydreams. But he couldn't help it. His mind replayed their conversations on a loop, and he couldn't wait to learn more about her.

His hands shook as Claire's car pulled into the gravel parking lot, and he strode over to meet her.

She stepped out of the car. "This is quite the spot, Marcus. I'm curious about what you have planned for tonight."

Marcus barely heard her over the hammering of his heart. She wore a flowing golden knee-length dress that accentuated her features. If Greek goddesses were real, Claire Lovery was one of them. Her makeup was subtle but enhanced her naturally beautiful face. He was awestruck and stood there gaping at her.

"Are you okay?" She quirked a perfect eyebrow and touched his arm.

"You're beautiful, Claire. Thank you for joining me tonight. I've been thinking about this all day." He smiled at her and handed her the bouquet before offering his arm.

"These are beautiful. Thank you so much. I've been looking forward to this night too."

After accepting his arm, Marcus led them to the dock and to the ladder at the end. He climbed down the ladder to the rowboat beneath. He held steady to the ladder and watched her follow after, even allowing him to hold her waist to help her down.

Once settled, Marcus pulled out a picnic basket and handed it to her.

Claire's eyebrows flicked up. "A picnic basket?"

He smiled and gripped the oars to begin the steady tread. "This will take about fifteen minutes so there are snacks inside for you."

Her full mouth curved upward and stole Marcus's breath. "You think of everything."

"I try. How was your day?"

She told him about the updates on Moxie and the other animals she'd treated as she munched on the cheese and grapes he packed.

Marcus loved every minute she spoke, and an easy smile planted on his mouth.

Midway, she stopped. "What are you smiling about?"

"You're even lovelier when you talk about your life. I'm enjoying it."

She smirked. "That's not a normal response from a man. I thought guys hate when their significant other drags on about their day?"

His face turned serious. "I couldn't be with you any other way."

A serene expression crossed her face, but she said nothing. He didn't mind as they rounded the curve of the river and arrived at their final destination.

A magnificent boat awaited them, glowing with candles he'd lit before meeting her at the dock. It even had fairy lights strewn across the top. A sweet melody from soft jazz welcomed them, completely in harmony with the lapping river around them.

"What is this?" Her mouth gaped, and he grinned.

"I called in a favor," he replied as they neared the back of the boat.

"One crazy favor! This boat is huge!" Her blue eyes glowed as they widened to take in all the details.

Marcus grinned as a blush heated his neck. "I dreamed our first official date would be a little more than just dinner. I appreciate everything you've done, and last night was different than anything I've ever experienced." He rubbed his neck, worried he rambled too much, but she surprised him with a shy smile.

"Last night was exceptional. I've never had that easy of a conversation with anyone. I'm glad I'm not the only one feeling that way."

Marcus tied the rowboat to the cleat on the boat and helped Claire up. When they both stood on the boat, Marcus held on a moment longer. He reached a hand up to brush a stray hair away from her face and smiled at her. "Last night was a night to remember and talking to you was the easiest feeling I've ever had. I've been thinking about you since the moment we met, and I look forward to each time I see you."

Claire's eyes glistened, and she leaned into his touch, encouraging him to hold her cheek. "I feel the same. It's been two days, but you haven't left my thoughts since. I admire you deeply, and I can't wait for the next time we see each other."

Marcus stepped forward and rested his free hand on her hip. Under the lights and the candles flickering around them, magic brewed in the breaths they shared. Closer they leaned toward each other, staring at each other with unblinking eyes.

"I've never felt this way so quickly ever," Marcus admitted as his heart thumped through his rib cage. "This all feels new to me, and I don't want to mess it up."

Claire's mouth twitched. "Not kissing me right now will be a mess up."

His body trembled with restraint at not kissing her, and he didn't wait a moment longer. He brushed his lips across hers with a gentle touch, but he lost all control when she made a small noise, and he roughly kissed her.

Pulling Claire against his body, he let his hand drift from her cheek to her hair and tugged her as close to his body as the space would allow. He tightened his hand against her hip, and she wrapped her arms around his neck before standing on her tiptoes.

Her perfume filled the air, and Marcus became intoxicated by Claire. The kiss lasted minutes, hours, or days; he didn't know how long it was before they broke apart, breathless.

Their eyes met and soft smiles stretched across their lips. He planted another gentle kiss on her lips before twining his hand through hers.

"I'm not messing this up, Claire Lovery. Allow me to hear more about your day over dinner."

Claire's answering grin lifted Marcus's heart, and he led them through the beginning of their first date, and they walked together right into the beginning of something new and beautiful.

EPILOGUE

And six months later, as they stood at the altar and said, "I do," Moxie stood behind Claire as her maid of honor, and Brownie stood next to him as best man.

Vinnie sniffled from behind a tissue in her seat on the second row, right behind their families. "I knew it," she'd whispered during the ceremony. "The moment I saw them together, I just knew…"

Sometimes, Marcus received accolades for having been willing to try to save Moxie, but it was Claire who did all the saving. She suffered his temper, fed it right back to him, and she'd still fallen in love with him. And Marcus would do whatever it took to keep it that way.

LAST CHANCE TO CLAIM YOUR FREE GIFT

Dear Reader -

Thanks for reading my book!

Sign up to my mailing list to receive exclusive copies of some of my future books as well as to be notified of any new releases, giveaways, contests, cover reveals and so much more.

Just click below to claim your free book and newsletter. See you soon...

www.MirandaRoseBarker.com/newsletter

LAST CHANCE TO CLAIM YOUR FREE GIFT

Miranda Rose Barker

REVIEW THIS BOOK!

Just visit the Amazon page for this book, scroll down to find and click the "Review this product" link in the *left-hand column*, right below existing Customer reviews.

Please share an honest review *(and, if you received an Advance Reader Copy (ARC) Team copy of the book, please say so in your Amazon review).*

Click Here to Review This Book

ALSO BY MIRANDA ROSE BARKER

Visit https://mirandarosebarker.com/mrbauthorpage
The Dog Lovers' Rescue Romance Series
The Very Human Dog Lover Story Series
The Tansy & Hank Pet Psychic Cozy Mystery Series
The Sycamore Grove Ghostly Cozy Mystery Series

OTHER DOG LOVER BOOKS
PUBLISHED BY CREATIVE
BOOKWORM PRESS:

Chew on Things, It Helps You Think: Words of Wisdom by a Worried Canine

Chew on Things Workbook for Fellow Worriers

COZY MYSTERIES BY MIRANDA ROSE BARKER

Visit https://mirandarosebarker.com/mrbauthorpage

The Sycamore Grove Ghostly Cozy Mystery Series

The Ghostly Visitation
If There's A Will, There's A Ghost
The Ghostly Treasure Hunt
The Ghostly Art of Flowers
The Scandalous School Mystery
The Persnickety Apparition Mystery

The Tansy & Hank Pet Psychic Cozy Mystery Series

The Foot in the Fountain Mystery
The Crystal Conundrum
The RV Riddle
The Curse of Pine Ridge
The Christmas Cookie Caper
The Baffling B and B Mystery
The Teapot Tempest Mystery
The Murder Map Mystery
A Rash of Murders Mystery
The Shocking Chalet Mystery

ABOUT THE AUTHOR

Miranda Rose Barker has enjoyed the company of dogs from the age of 7. She only later discovered the rewarding world of dog rescues in her mid-30's and since then, has lived with eight rescue dogs, including large and small mixed breeds from German shepherds to doodle dogs and some purebreds (schnauzers and other terriers).

A lifelong writer, she began writing fiction in 2000 and has loved bringing rescue dogs and their humans together in her books for years. She also delights in reading and writing cozy mysteries, usually ones with an amusing dog character.

Miranda Rose lives in southern California where she is often out looking for the next rescue pup to add to her own pack or a friend's pack.

Check out more of Miranda Rose Barker's latest titles in her book series: *The Sycamore Grove Ghostly Cozy Mystery Series*, *The Tansy & Hank Pet Psychic Cozy Mystery Series*, *The Dog Lovers' Rescue Romance Series*, *The Very Human Dog Lover Story Series*, *The Dogs Are Family Too Series*, and more.

Visit Miranda Rose Barker's Amazon Author Page or visit https://author.to/mirandarosebarkerbooks to learn more about her books and book series…

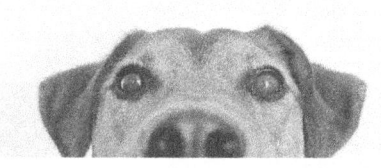

CPSIA information can be obtained
at www.ICGtesting.com
Printed in the USA
BVHW041756230223
659100BV00006B/200